ents

edgment is given authors, publishers, photographers, museums, and agents
reprint the following copyrighted material. Every effort has been made to
ght owners. In case of any omissions, the Publisher will be pleased to make
edgments in future editions.

urday by E. L. Konigsburg. This edition is reprinted by arrangement with
s For Young Readers, Simon & Schuster Children's Publishing Division.
6 by E. L. Konigsburg. All rights reserved.

y Joyce Hansen, from *Lost and Found*. Copyright © 2000 by M. Jerry Weiss
eiss. Reprinted by permission of Tom Doherty Associates.

n www.seaworld.org. Reprinted by permission.

" by Karina Snow, "Change for a Dollar" by Bonnie Maloney and "So How Do
" by Margaret Hill, from *Chicken Soup for the Teenage Soul II*, copyright © 1998
Mark Victor Hansen and Kimberly Kirberger. Reprinted by permission of
ications, Inc.

at Kneel Down Like Elephants," from *Words Like Pain and Fear* by Karen Fiser.
2 by Karen Fiser. Reprinted by permission of Zoland Books, Cambridge,

d *Table With Chinese Teapot*, 1945, Anne Redpath. Oil on canvas. Private
Bridgeman Art Library.

McGraw-Hill

Division of The **McGraw·Hill** Companies

to:

v-Hill

3240

2-1
ted States of America
4 03

The Vie
Satur

with Related

Acknowledgm

Grateful acknow
for permission t
determine copy
suitable acknow

The View from
Atheneum Boc
Copyright © 1

"A Safe Space'
and Hellen S.

"Sea Turtles" fi

"An A for Mrs
You Boost an E
by Jack Canfie
Health Comm

"Wheelchairs
Copyright © 1
Massachusetts

Cover Art: *R*
Collection/Th

Glencoe

Glenco
McGra

New York, New York   Columbus, Ohio   Woodl

Contents

The View from Saturday

Continued

Contents *Continued*

Related Readings 117

The View from Saturday

E. L. Konigsburg

One

Mrs. Eva Marie Olinski always gave good answers. Whenever she was asked how she had selected her team for the Academic Bowl, she chose one of several good answers. Most often she said that the four members of her team had skills that balanced one another. That was reasonable. Sometimes she said that she knew her team would practice. That was accurate. To the district superintendent of schools, she gave a bad answer, but she did that only once, only to him, and if that answer was not good, her reason for giving it was.

The fact was that Mrs. Olinski did not know how she had chosen her team, and the further fact was that she didn't know that she didn't know until she did know. Of course, that is true of most things: you do not know up to and including the very last second before you do. And for Mrs. Olinski that was not until Bowl Day was over and so was the work of her four sixth graders.

They called themselves The Souls. They told Mrs. Olinski that they were The Souls long before they were a team, but she told them that they were a team as soon as they became The Souls. Then after a while, teacher and team agreed that they were arguing chicken-or-egg. Whichever way it began—chicken-or-egg, team-or-The Souls—it definitely ended with an egg. Definitely, an egg.

People still remark about how extraordinary it was to have four sixth graders make it to the finals. There had been a few seventh graders scattered among the other teams, but all the rest of the middle school regional champs were eighth graders. Both of the Maxwell boys' voices had deepened, and the girls displayed lacy bra straps inside their T-shirt necklines. The fact that the necklines were outsized and that the two pairs of straps matched—they were apricot-colored—made Mrs. Olinski believe that they were not making a fashion statement as much as they were saying something. To her four sixth graders puberty was something they could spell and define but had yet to experience.

Unlike football bowls, there had been no season tallies for the academic teams. There had been no best-of-five. Each contest had been an elimination round. There were winners, and there were losers. From the start, the rule was: Lose one game, and you are out.

* * *

So it was on Bowl Day.

At the start of the day, there had been eight regional champs. Now there were two—Epiphany and Maxwell.

It was afternoon by the time they got to the last round, and Mrs. Olinski sat shivering in a windowless room in a building big enough and official enough to have its own zip code. This was Albany, the capital of the state of New York. This was the last Saturday in May, and some robot—human or electronic—had checked the calendar instead of the weather report and had turned on the air-conditioning. Like everyone else in the audience, Mrs. Olinski wore a short-sleeved T-shirt with her team's logo across the front. Maxwell's were navy; Epiphany's were red and were as loud as things were permitted to get in that large, cold room. The audience had been asked not to whistle, cheer, stomp, hold up signs, wave banners, or even applaud. They were reminded that this Bowl was for brains, not brawn, and decorum— something between chapel and classroom—was the order of the day.

Epiphany sat on one side of a long table; Maxwell, the other. At a lectern between them stood the commissioner of education of the state of New York. He smiled benevolently over the audience as he reached inside his inner breast pocket and withdrew a pair of reading glasses. With a flick of his wrist he opened them and put them on.

Mrs. Olinski hugged her upper arms and wondered if maybe it was nerves and not the quartering wind blowing from the ceiling vents that was causing her shivers. She watched with bated (and visible) breath as the commissioner placed his hand into a large clear glass bowl. His college class ring knocked bottom. (Had the room been two degrees colder, the glass would have shattered.) He withdrew a piece of paper, unfolded it, and read, "What is the meaning of the word *calligraphy* and from what language does it derive?"

A buzzer sounded.

Mrs. Olinski knew whose it was. She was sure of it. She leaned back and relaxed. She was not nervous. Excited, yes. Nervous, no.

The television lights glanced off Noah Gershom's glasses. He had been the first chosen.

Noah Writes a B & B Letter

My mother insisted that I write a B & B letter to my grandparents. I told her that I could not write a B & B letter, and she asked me why, and I told her that I did not know what a B & B letter was. She explained—not too patiently—that a B & B letter is a *bread and butter letter* you write to people to thank them for having you as their houseguest. I told her that I was taught never to use the word you are defining in its definition and that she ought to think of a substitute word for *letter* if she is defining it. Mother then made a remark about how Western Civilization was in a decline because people of my generation knew how to nitpick but not how to write a B & B letter.

I told her that, with all due respect, I did not think I owed Grandma and Grandpa a B & B. And then I stated my case. Fact: I was not just a houseguest, I was family; and fact: I had not been their houseguest by choice because fact: She had sent me to them because she had won a cruise for selling more houses in Epiphany than anyone else in the world and if she had shared her cruise with Joey and me instead of with her husband, my father, I would not have been sent to Florida in the first place and fact: She, not me, owed them thanks; and further fact: I had been such a wonderful help while I was there that Grandma and Grandpa would probably want to write me a B & B.

My brother Joey had been sent to my other set of grandparents, who live in a normal suburb in Connecticut. "Is Joey writing a B & B to Grandma and Grandpa Eberle?"

"Even as we speak," Mother replied.

"Well, maybe he has something to be thankful for," I said.

Mother drew in her breath as if she were about to say something else about what children of my generation were doing to Western Civilization, but instead, she said, "Write," and closed my bedroom door behind her. I opened the door and called out to her, "Can I use the computer?"

She said, "I know you can use the computer, Noah, but you *may* not." I was about to make a remark about who was nitpicking now, but Mother gave me such a negative look that I knew any thoughts I had had better be about bread and butter and not nitpicking.

I gazed at my closed bedroom door and then out the window. Door. Window. Door. Window. There was no escape.

I took a box of notepaper out of my desk drawer. The notes were bigger than postage stamps, but not by much. I took out a ballpoint pen and started pressing it against a piece of scrap paper, making dents in the paper but not making a mark. Ballpoint pens sometimes take a while to get started. When I was down in Florida, Tillie Nachman had said, "The ballpoint pen has been the biggest single factor in the decline of Western Civilization. It makes the written word cheap, fast, and totally without character." My mother and Tillie should get together. Between them, they have come up with the two major reasons why Western Civilization is about to collapse.

Not because I was trying to save Western Civilization but because I wanted to actually get my B & B letter written, I put the ballpoint pen back into the drawer and took out my calligraphy pen, the one that uses wet ink. I didn't fill it. I would fill it when I was ready to write. I also took out a sharpened pencil and a pad of Post-it notes to jot down any ideas that might come to mind.

I wrote *red wagon*. The red wagon had definitely been a gift— even though, under the circumstances, I didn't bring it back to Epiphany with me. I thought a while longer and wrote *tuxedo T-shirt*. It, too, had been a gift, but I didn't have that either. I wrote *calligraphy pen and bottle of ink*. A wet ink pen and a bottle of ink had been given to me, but the ones I took out of my desk drawer were ones I had bought myself. The calligraphy pen made me remember about the Post-it notes I had bought to correct the problem that had developed with the ink. Even though I had bought the Post-it notes myself, I added *Post-it notes* to my list. I peeled off the Post-it note containing my list and stuck it on the wall in front of my desk, and then, as my mother had commanded, I thought again.

Century Village where my Gershom grandparents live is not like any place I had ever been to. It is in Florida, but it is not exactly Disney World or Sea World or other regular destinations. It is like a theme park for old people. Almost everyone who lives there is retired from useful life. Grandma Sadie and Grandpa Nate fit in nicely.

It all started when Margaret Draper and Izzy Diamondstein decided to get married, and the citizens of Century Village called a meeting in the clubhouse to organize the wedding.

In their former lives, Grandma Sadie and Grandpa Nate had owned a small bakery right here in Epiphany, New York, so Grandma volunteered to do the wedding cake, and Grandpa Nate, whose chief hobby had always been violin playing, promised to arrange for the music.

My grandfather Gershom began practicing immediately and often. Grandma Sadie said, "Nathan, how can you stand playing the same piece over and over again?" And Grandpa Nate answered, "Why don't you ask me how I can stand making love to the same woman over and over again?" And even though she is the age she is, my grandmother blushed and said, *Sha! a shanda far die kinder*, a remark I had heard many times before Grandma and Grandpa moved to Century Village. Translated it means, "Hush up, it's a shame for the children," but what it really meant was that Grandpa was embarrassing Grandma.

Mr. Cantor, a retired postman from Pennsylvania, who was devoted to growing orchids, said that he would have enough blossoms for the corsages. And Mrs. Kerchmer said that she would lend her African violets for the centerpieces.

Tillie Nachman volunteered to do the invitations, and Rabbi Friedman, who was a rabbi in his former life, said he would perform the ceremony even though Margaret Draper was not Jewish and Izzy Diamondstein was. This was a late second marriage, and there wouldn't be any concern about what religion they should choose for their children since all their children were already grown up and chosen. Grandpa Nate later explained to me that unlike the average citizen of Century Village, rabbis don't have former lives. They are what they were; once a rabbi, always a rabbi.

Many citizens of Century Village were widows who had once been great family cooks, so they formed a committee to plan the wedding dinner. Everyone agreed to share the cost, and they made up a menu and a master shopping list.

After that first meeting, Grandpa Nate and I took Tillie Nachman, a former New York City person who had never learned to drive, to the stationery store so that she could buy the invitations. While she shopped for the invitations, Grandpa and I went to Wal-Mart to pick up Grandma's prescription, and that is when we saw the red wagon special. Grandpa bought it for me, and it's a good thing he did. It came in handy until Allen came along.

I checked my list. *Post-it notes*. I had bought them when we ran out of invitations. Of course, we didn't run out of invitations until Tillie's cat got its paws into the ink.

Tillie was filling in the *who-what-when-and-where* on the invitations when I noticed that she had the prettiest handwriting I had ever seen. "Calligraphy," she said. "It means beautiful writing," and she asked me if I would like to learn how to write like her. I said yes. She said she would give me lessons if I would help her address the envelopes. So Grandpa drove us to an art supply store where she bought me a calligraphy pen and a bottle of ink. It was while Tillie was trying out various pen points (called *nibs*) that she made the remark about the ballpoint pen being the biggest single factor in the decline of Western Civilization.

After choosing a nib Tillie said, "I hope in the future, Noah, that you will use a ballpoint pen only when you have to press hard to make multiple carbons."

I couldn't promise that. There were times in school when a person had to do things fast, cheap, and without character.

Tillie said, "There are pens that come with ink in a cartridge, Noah, but I will have nothing to do with them." So when we were back at her condo, Tillie taught me how to fill a pen, or, as she said, "How to *properly* fill a pen."

One: Turn the filling plunger counterclockwise as far as it will go. Two: Dip the nib completely into the ink. Three: Turn the filling plunger clockwise until it stops. Four: Hold the nib above the ink bottle and turn the plunger counterclockwise again until three drops of ink fall back into the bottle. Five: Turn the plunger clockwise to stop the drops. Six: Wipe the excess ink completely from pen and nib.

When I told Tillie that six steps seemed a lot to have to do before you begin, she said, "You must think of those six steps not as preparation for the beginning but as the beginning itself."

I practiced my calligraphy. I practiced all twenty-six letters of the alphabet, including X, which was not part of any of the who-what-when-and-wheres or any of the addresses but is a very good letter to practice because fact: It is not easy.

When Tillie decided that I was good enough to help with the invitations, I sat on the floor of her living room and used her coffee table as my desk. She sat at the kitchen table. Fact: Many of the domiciles in Century Village do not have family rooms with desks.

There was a lot of writing to do because at the bottom of each and every one of those invitations, we wrote: Your presence but no presents. Tillie said that practically all the invitations that went out from Century Village said that. "Besides," she said, "I think that making the wedding is enough of a present."

I was doing a wonderful job until Thomas Stearns, called T. S., Tillie's cat, pounced into my lap, and I jumped up and spilled the ink, and the cat walked through the spilled ink and onto a couple of the invitations I was addressing. A few—five altogether—now had cat's paws.

Tillie was pretty upset because she had not bought extras because she said, "I don't make mistakes." In her former life Tillie had been a bookkeeper. I heard her say, "I can add up a column of figures with the best of them." I didn't know if she meant the best of the computers or the best of the bookkeepers, and I didn't ask because I was afraid I already knew.

I told Tillie not to worry. I told her that I would think of something. And I did. That's when I bought the Post-it notes. I put a Post-it into each of the invitations that had a cat's paw mark. On the Post-it I wrote (in faultless calligraphy): Bring this specially marked invitation to the wedding and receive a surprise gift. When Tillie asked me what the surprise would be, I told her not to worry, that I would think of something. And I did. But fact: It wasn't easy.

On the day the groceries were to be purchased, the citizens of Century Village formed their version of the Home Shopping network. They met in the clubhouse again. Everyone sat in rows, holding coupons they'd clipped since printing began. They asked me to be master of ceremonies.

I sat at a table in front of the clubhouse room and called out items from the master grocery list. It was a lot like a game of Go Fish. I said, "I need one Crisco, four margarines, *pareve*, and let's have all your paper towels." Everyone searched through their fistfuls of coupons and gave me the ones that were needed. Tillie circled the items we had coupons for.

Then we checked the newspaper for supermarket specials and made out lists for each of the stores, depending on which one had the best buy in a particular item. I wrote the Gershom list in calligraphy. It didn't slow things down too much, and the citizens of Century Village are accustomed to waiting.

Later that day, everyone returned to the clubhouse with the groceries and the store receipts. Tillie added, divided, and straightened out who owed and who was owed, and no one bothered to check because everyone knew that Tillie Nachman did not make mistakes. Then we had to check the grocery list against the menu and who was cooking what. I helped distribute the groceries to the proper households, using the new red wagon.

Fact: I did a wonderful job.

On the day of the wedding I was in great demand to take things over to the clubhouse in my wagon. The African violets alone took three trips, and the briskets took two. Next, Mr. Cantor and I delivered the orchid corsages to the bride and her maid of honor. In the real world, I had never met anyone who spent as much time with flowers as Mr. Cantor. Mrs. Draper's maid of honor was to be her daughter, Mrs. Potter. Mrs. Draper used to live in my hometown, which is Epiphany, New York, and her daughter, Mrs. Potter, still does. Mrs. Potter bought a new dress and flew down for the wedding, but we didn't fly down together. I had come weeks before—my first trip as an unaccompanied minor.

Mr. Cantor and I took flowers over to the groom and his best man to put in their buttonholes. Allen, who was Izzy Diamondstein's son, was to be best man. They both live in Florida and have the same last name.

Allen Diamondstein still lived in the real world because even though he was Izzy's child and even though he was full-grown, he was too young to live in Century Village. Fact: Allen Diamondstein was the most nervous human being I have ever seen in my entire life. Fact: His wife had left him. She had moved to Epiphany and taken a job with my father, who is the best dentist in town (fact).

Allen Diamondstein kept saying, "Isn't it ironic? My father is getting married just as I am getting divorced." This was not the greatest conversation starter in the world. No one knew what to say after he said it. Some cleared their throats and said nothing. Others cleared their throats and changed the subject.

I must have heard him say it a dozen times, and I never knew what to say either. At first I wondered if that was because I didn't know the meaning of *ironic*. So I looked it up.

The meaning that best fits (and does not use the same word in its definition) is "the contrast between what you expect to happen and what really happens." But after I looked it up, I couldn't figure out what was ironic about Allen Diamondstein's getting divorced and Izzy Diamondstein's getting married. The way Allen Diamondstein acted, I can tell you that divorce would be the only possible thing you could expect from marriage to him. And the way Izzy acted around Margaret, marriage would not only be expected, it would be necessary. *Sha! a shanda far die kinder.* They were embarrassing to watch, but not so embarrassing that I didn't.

Wedding cakes are not baked as much as they are built. In the real world, people don't build wedding cakes. They order in. If you are going to build it yourself, it is not done in a day. It takes three. On the first day, Grandma Sadie baked the layers. On the second, she constructed the cake, using cardboard bases and straws for supports, and made the basic icing to cover the layers. On the third day, she made the designer icing for the rosebuds and put the little bride and groom on the top. Fact: The cake was beautiful.

Fortunately, Grandpa Nate took its picture right after she finished it, so Grandma Sadie can remember how it looked for a little while.

Allen Diamondstein would tell you that the red wagon was the problem, but I would say that it's ironic that he should say so. It definitely wasn't. He was. How else were we supposed to deliver the cake to the clubhouse? It was too tall to fit in the trunk of the car, and since on an average day the outside temperature in Century Village is body temperature, there would be a major meltdown before the cake got to the clubhouse where the wedding was to take place. That's when I got the idea to load up the wagon with ice, put a sheet of plastic over the ice, put the cake on top of that, and slowly wheel it over there, with me pulling and Grandpa checking the rear.

Grandpa Nate went to the Jiffy store and bought three bags of ice, and we loaded them into the wagon. Too much. Since we didn't want the bed of the wagon filled right up to the edge, we emptied some, dumping it out on the cement of the patio. That's where we were going to load the wagon so we wouldn't have to wheel the wagon down any steps to get it to the meeting room.

Just after we loaded the cake onto the wagon, Allen Diamondstein came over to Grandma's. He said his father wanted him to pick up a prayer book, but I think his father sent him because he was making the groom nervous.

No one answered when he rang the front doorbell because we were all in the back loading the cake into the red wagon, so he walked around back to the patio. Unfortunately, he didn't see the wagon handle, so he tripped on it, slid on the wet concrete, fell in the puddle of melted ice and, unfortunately, toppled the wedding cake.

The little top layer was totally smashed; it fell in the same puddle as Allen, and the little bride and groom were seriously maimed.

So was Allen's ankle. Which fact I detected when he grabbed his foot and started to moan while still sitting in the puddle on the patio. Grandpa Nate called 911. Grandma Sadie returned to the kitchen to whip up a repair batch of icing. Grandpa Nate took the remains of the cake to the clubhouse, and I sat with Allen until the ambulance came. He was not good company.

The groom called to see what was taking Allen so long. I answered the phone, and I thought I would have to call 911 for him, too. "Don't panic," I said. "I'll be your best man."

I did not tell Izzy what had happened to the couple on top of the wedding cake because people get very superstitious at weddings and no one wants a wounded bride and groom sitting on top of the cake with which they are to start a happy marriage. I had seen that sort of thing often enough in the movies: A close-up of the shattered little bride and groom floating in a puddle of melted ice signifying the fate of the real bride and groom. So although I had to tell Izzy Diamondstein what had happened to Allen, I didn't say a word about the top of the wedding cake. I didn't think I could convince him that having the little bride and groom fall into a puddle was ironic.

He seemed to calm down when I volunteered to be best man, which was about the same time that we found out from the ambulance driver that Allen would be back at Century Village in time for the wedding even if he probably wouldn't be able to walk down the aisle.

As soon as the ambulance took Allen away, I ran over to Mr. Cantor's place and asked him to please, please find another orchid for the top of the cake although it would be better if he could find two since the second layer was now the top layer and was bigger. Mr. Cantor found two beautiful sprays of orchids, which Grandma Sadie artistically arranged around the new top layer.

Since I had promised to be best man, not having a tux was a problem. I couldn't fit in Allen's, not that I would have wanted to if I could. That's when Grandpa Nate called Bella Dubinsky.

In her former life, Bella had been an artist. She painted the pictures that went into the pattern books for people who sew their own clothes. In the real world I never met anyone who sewed her own clothes, but in Century Village, I had met three. Bella had a supply of fabric paints, and within two hours we had painted a T-shirt that looked like a tuxedo with a red bow tie. I say *we* because I helped color in the lines she drew. It's not easy filling in the lines on T-shirt material; it scrunches up under the weight of the brush, leaving skip marks. You have to go over it again and again. Fortunately, the paints dry fast and by four o'clock, it was ready to wear.

Repaired, the wedding cake looked beautiful. If Allen had not told, no one would have guessed that those orchids didn't belong on top. But Allen told. He told everyone. He also apologized for my being best man. I didn't think that I was someone he had to apologize for. I had helped a lot, and I looked totally presentable in my tuxedo T-shirt, which was a real work of art.

Fact: Being best man is not hard. You walk down the aisle with the maid of honor. Who, in this case, was a matron of honor because she is married. I admit that having the son of the groom, Allen, as best man would have been a better match, size-wise, for the daughter of the bride even though one is married and the other divorced, but the essential fact is that I did a very good job. I stood beside the groom. Mrs. Potter stood beside the bride, and the four of us stood in front of the rabbi, and all five of us stood under the bridal canopy, which I know is called a *chupah* and which I think is spelled the way I spelled it. I didn't yawn, sneeze, or scratch any visible thing. I held the wedding ring until the rabbi nodded, and I handed it over.

I did an excellent job of being best man even though when I was under the chupah, I was under a lot of pressure trying to think of surprises for the cat's paw invitations. The idea came to me at the very moment Izzy smashed the glass and everyone yelled *mazel tov*. Even before Izzy stopped kissing the bride, I knew what I could do. (Fact: It was a very long and thorough kiss.)

It wouldn't be easy. It would mean giving up things I loved, but I had to do it.

When everyone except Allen was dancing the *hora*, I slipped out of the clubhouse and ran back to Grandma Sadie's. I took off my tuxedo T-shirt, folded it nicely, and put it in my red wagon. I found the package of Post-it notes, my calligraphy pen, and bottle of ink and after making sure that the ink was tightly closed, I put those in the wagon, too. When I returned to the wedding party, the dance was over, and everyone was sitting around looking exhausted. My moment had arrived.

I tapped a glass with a spoon as I had seen grown-ups do, and I said, "Ladies and gentlemen, will those lucky few who have the specially marked invitations, please come forward. It is time to choose your surprise gift." I saw them pick up their cat's-paw invitations and walk over to the band where I was standing beside my red wagon. "First," I said, "we have one hand-painted T-shirt, which is an original work of art done by Mrs. Bella Dubinsky. In addition, we have a calligraphy pen, almost new, and bottle of ink, almost full. These are the perfect instruments for beautiful handwriting. We have one packet of Post-it notes, complete except for five." I swallowed hard and added, "And we have one red wagon."

Tillie Nachman, who could count precisely, said, "But that's only four gifts, and there were five cat's-paw invitations."

"Oh, yes," I said, "the fifth gift is the best of all."

Everyone asked at once, *Whatisit? Whatisit? Whatisit?*

I sucked in my breath until my lungs felt like twin dirigibles inside my ribs. "The best gift of all is . . . the very best . . . the very best gift of all is . . . to give up your gift."

A thick silence fell over the room. Then Tillie Nachman started clapping. Soon the others joined in, and I noticed Grandma Sadie and Grandpa Nate looking proud.

At first everyone who held a cat's-paw invitation wanted to be the one to give up his gift, but I did not want that. If they didn't take my presents, I would feel as if they didn't matter. Mr. Cantor stepped forward and took the Post-it notes. He said he could use them for labeling his plants. He said that he was donating an orchid plant as the fifth gift. Then Tillie promised calligraphy lessons to the person who took the pen and ink, and Bella promised fabric paint-ing lessons to the person who took the tuxedo T-shirt. In that way each of my gifts kept on giving.

Four cat's-paw gifts were now taken.

Only the red wagon remained. Guess who had the fifth cat's-paw invitation?

Allen, the son of.

Allen said he didn't want the little red wagon. He said that he had no use for a wagon in the real world where he was an accountant.

When Izzy, the groom, rose from the table to make a toast, he lifted his glass of wine and said, "Margy and I want to thank all our friends in Century Village. We don't know if we can ever thank you enough for giving our life together this wonderful start. As you know, Margy and I have pooled our resources and bought a little condo on the ocean. Not exactly *on* the ocean. It is, after all, a high-rise. We will miss the community life here, but we don't want to miss our friends. We'll visit. We want you to visit us. Our wel-come mat is out. Always. We leave many memories behind. And we are also leaving this little red wagon. Every time you use it, please think of this happy occasion."

Izzy started to sit down, but halfway he got up again and added, "Consider it a gift to everyone from the best man." He never said which best man he meant, but I'm pretty sure he meant me.

Now back in the real world, I sat at my desk and crossed every single item off the list. I didn't have the wagon, the Post-it notes, the T-shirt that Bella Dubinsky had designed, or the pen and ink that Tillie Nachman had bought me. I did have a new pad of Post-it notes and a new calligraphy pen—both of which I had bought with my own money when I got back to Epiphany.

I never had to write a B & B letter when we stayed at Disney

World or Sea World. Of course, Century Village is not exactly Disney World or Sea World either. Century Village is not like any other place in Western Civilization. It is not like any other place in the entire world.

I picked up my pen and filled it *properly*, the six-step process that Tillie had taught me. She had said, "You must think of those six steps not as preparation for the beginning but as the beginning itself." I knew then that I had started my B & B. I let my pen drink up a whole plunger full of ink and then holding the pen over the bottle, I squeezed three drops back into the bottle.

And I thought—a B & B letter is giving just a few drops back to the bottle. I put away the tiny notepad and took out a full sheet of calligraphy paper and began,

> *Dear Grandma Sadie and Grandpa Nate,*
> *Thank you for a vacation that was out of this*
> *world . . .*

Two

THE CONTEST HAD WARMED UP, and so had Mrs. Olinski. From her seat on the aisle she waited.

On her left sat Dr. Roy Clayton Rohmer, the District Superintendent for Clarion County. Both Dr. Rohmer and Mrs. Olinski paid strict attention to the commissioner, the man at the podium. There could be no mistake: This was the man of the hour, king for the day.

He wore a navy blue, precision fit pin-striped suit and a white-on-dazzling-white shirt. An edge of his French cuffs showed beneath his jacket sleeves. Mrs. Olinski was not sure how much the correct amount was, but she knew that if she put a spirit-level to his, they would be exactly right. The French cuffs were held together with onyx cuff links, and his collar was tied with a red-striped power necktie. The television lights beamed down on his crown of hair, which was tinted the color of peach pits. He was dressed, brushed, coiffed, and blow-dried not just to be seen but to be looked at.

Dr. Rohmer could not, would not take his eyes off the man at the podium, and Mrs. Olinski thought of *Alice in Wonderland*. "Don't look at me like that!" said the king to the Cheshire Cat. "A cat may look at a king," said Alice. Mrs. Olinski wanted to tell Dr. Rohmer that a cat may look at a king. But why bother? The audience was not permitted to speak.

* * *

After The Souls had won the Epiphany Middle School championship, Dr. Roy Clayton Rohmer paid a visit to Mrs. Olinski and asked—guess what?—why had she chosen this team. She still did not know (and wouldn't until after it was all over), but by that time the success of The Souls (even if she did not yet know that they were The Souls) had made Mrs. Olinski less timid.

Dr. Rohmer had announced that he had just completed a three-day workshop on multiculturalism for *ed-you-kay-toars*. Mrs. Olinski had always been amused by educators who called themselves *ed-you-kay-toars*. So, when he asked her how she had chosen the four members of her academic team, Mrs. Olinski knitted her brow and answered with hushed seriousness. "In the interest of diversity," she said, "I chose a brunette, a redhead, a blond, and a kid with hair as black as print on paper."

Dr. Rohmer was not amused. He gave Mrs. Olinski a capsule lecture on what multiculturalism really means.

"Oh," she said, "then we're still safe, Dr. Rohmer. You can tell the taxpayers that the Epiphany Middle School team has one Jew, one half-Jew, a WASP, and an Indian."

"Jews, half-Jews, and WASPs have nothing to do with diversity, Mrs. Olinski. The Indian does. But we don't call them Indians anymore. We call them Native Americans."

"Not this one," she replied.

"Mrs. Olinski," Dr. Rohmer asked, "would you like it if people called you a cripple?"

Mrs. Olinski gave up. Everyone believed that she could be wounded by the word *cripple*. She could never explain to Dr. Rohmer, nor would she try to, that the word itself does not hurt, but the manner of its delivery can. For all of his training, Dr. Rohmer would never believe that cripples themselves are a diverse group, and some make jokes.

Nadia was the redhead of Mrs. Olinski's diverse group.

Had she been born five hundred years sooner, Raphael would have chosen her as a model for his cherubs. Tendrils of bright red hair framed her face, a spray of freckles powdered her nose, and she was as plump as a perfectly ripened peach. Raphael probably would have painted out the freckles, and that would have been a mistake. Like brushing the cinnamon off cinnamon toast.

For the first few weeks of the new school year, Nadia hardly spoke. All the sixth graders—like Mrs. Olinski herself—were new to Epiphany Middle School, but Nadia—like Mrs. Olinski herself— seemed most disconnected. Both were watchers and waiters, cautious about being friendly, about showing themselves.

Then on the middle Monday in October, Nadia Diamondstein arrived in class with a smile and addressed her teacher. "Don't you think, Mrs. Olinski, that autumn is the most glorious time of year?" Mrs. Olinski confessed that it was her favorite season and told Nadia that she sometimes felt guilty because she thought she ought to prefer spring, with its pledge to make the lilies bloom again.

Every morning thereafter, Nadia smiled as she entered class and greeted Mrs. Olinski with a word from her southern past. She said, "Hey."

Mrs. Olinski knew that Nadia Diamondstein was not only incandescently beautiful but was also a star.

* * *

The commissioner of education picked up the next question. Looking over the rims of his reading glasses, he slowly unfolded the paper. "This question has two parts," he said. "To receive credit, you must answer both parts." Lowering his eyes, he read, "What is the name given to that portion of the North Atlantic Ocean that is noted for its abundance of seaweed, and what is its importance to the ecology of our planet?"

Nadia Diamondstein rang in.

Nadia Tells of Turtle Love

My grandfather is a slim person of average height with heavy, heathery-gray eyebrows. He lives in a high-rise condominium on the beach in Florida. He lives there with his new wife whom he calls Margy. I was told to call her Margaret, not Aunt Margaret or Mrs. Diamondstein. It sounded disrespectful to me—calling a woman old enough to be my grandmother by her first name, but I did as I was told.

Last summer, just before my grandfather married Margaret, my mother and father got divorced, and Mother moved the two of us to upstate New York where she had grown up. She said that she needed some autumn in her life. I had never thought that I would see autumn in New York or anywhere else because even when we vacationed at a place that had one, we always had to return for school before it started. In Florida school starts before Labor Day. Whatever it says on the calendar, Florida has de facto summer.

Dividing up my time was part of the divorce settlement. I was to spend Thanksgiving, spring vacation, and one month over the summer with Dad. He left Christmas holidays for Mother because it is her holiday, not his. I am the product of a mixed marriage.

This first summer of their separation, Dad chose August for his visitation rights. He picked us up early Friday evening. *Us* means Ginger and me. Ginger is my dog. I do not know who was happier to see me at the airport—Dad or Ginger. The worst part of the trip had been checking Ginger into the baggage compartment.

Dad always was a nervous person, but since the divorce he had become terminally so. He was having a difficult time adjusting to being alone. He had sold the house that we lived in when we were a family and had moved into a swinging singles apartment complex, but my father could no more swing than a gate on rusty hinges.

For the first day and a half after I arrived, Dad hovered over me like the Goodyear blimp over the Orange Bowl. He did not enjoy the hovering, and I did not enjoy being hovered, but he did not know what to do with me, and I did not know what to tell him, except to tell him to stop hovering, which seemed to be the only thing he knew how to do.

On Sunday we went to see Grandpa Izzy and Margaret.

Grandpa Izzy was happy to see me. Under those bushy eyebrows of his, Grandpa Izzy's eyes are bright blue like the sudden underside of a bird wing. His eyes have always been the most alive part of him, but when Bubbe Frieda died, they seemed to die, too. Since he married Margaret though, they seem bright enough to give off light of their own. He is sixty-nine years old, and he is in love.

Margaret is a short blonde. She is very different from my bubbe but not very different from the thousands who make their home in South Florida. There are so many blond widows in the state of Florida, and they are all so much alike, they ought to have a kennel breed named and registered for them. Like all the others, Margaret dresses atrociously. She wears pastel-colored pantsuits with elastic waists or white slacks with overblouses of bright, bold prints. She carries her eyeglasses—blue-rimmed bifocals—on a gold metal chain around her neck. They all do. Margaret is not fat, but she certainly is not slim. She is thick around the middle, and when she wears her green polyester pantsuit, she looks like a Granny Smith apple. Grandpa Izzy would say Delicious.

Grandpa Izzy and Margaret are like Jack-Sprat-could-eat-no-fat and his wife-could-eat-no-lean. Grandpa Izzy says that Margaret is *zaftig*, which is Yiddish for pleasingly plump. Everything about her pleases him. He seems to find it difficult to keep himself from pinching her or pinching himself for having the good fortune to find and marry her. Such public displays of affection can be embarrassing to a pre-pubescent girl like me who is not accustomed to being in the company of two married people who like each other.

On Sunday we went out for brunch at one of those mammoth places where the menu is small and the portions are large, and every senior citizen leaves with a Styrofoam box containing leftovers. We had to wait to be seated at the restaurant because Sunday brunch is a major social custom in Florida retirement communities. Dad twice asked the restaurant hostess how much longer we would have to wait. Grandpa Izzy and Margaret tried to tell Dad that they did not mind waiting since visiting with each other was part of the plan, and they did not mind doing it at the restaurant. But hovering at low altitudes seemed to be my father's new best thing.

When we were finally seated, we had a nice enough time. Margaret had Belgian waffles and did not require a Styrofoam box for leftovers because there were none; she ate everything that was on her plate—strawberry preserves, pseudo whipped cream and all. She did not order decaf coffee but drank three cups of regular.

Margaret was not at all curious about me. I thought she would want to know how I liked our new home, which is in Epiphany, the very town she had lived in before she moved to Florida. Maybe she thought that I was not curious about her because I did not ask her about her wedding, which neither Mother nor I attended. But I believe that the grown-up should ask the questions first, and besides, Mother and I had gotten a full report on the wedding from Noah Gershom who, due to unforeseen circumstances, had been best man. I did not find Noah's account of the events surrounding his becoming best man quite as amusing as he did, but for several complicated reasons, I did not express my opinion.

One of the complications was that my mother works for Dr. Gershom, who is Noah's father. My mother is a dental hygienist by profession, and Dr. Gershom is a dentist. One of the reasons we moved to Epiphany was that Mother got a job there. My mother happens to be an excellent hygienist, and Dr. Gershom was lucky to get her, but nevertheless, I thought it best not to tell Noah Gershom that his account of my grandfather's wedding was not as amusing as he thought it was.

Dad's new apartment complex was miles away from our old neighborhood. I called two of my former friends, but getting together with them was not easy. Our schedules, which had once matched, seemed to be in different time zones now. Geography made the difference.

When we finally got together, I thought we would have fun. We did not. Either I had changed, or they had changed, or all of us had. I would not try again. I concluded that many friendships are born and maintained for purely geographical reasons. I preferred Ginger.

Work seemed to be the only thing that held Dad together, but leaving me alone that week while he went to the office made him feel guilty and ended up making him even more nervous, if such a thing were possible. I spent part of my time at the apartment complex pool, which was almost empty during the day. I read and watched talk shows and took Ginger on walks around the golf course that bordered the swinging singles complex. I enjoyed not having Dad hover over me, but I did not tell him so.

Grandpa Izzy called every day. He volunteered to come to swinging singles to pick me up after Dad left for work and after the morning rush-hour traffic. All the retirees in South Florida wait for the rush-hour traffic to be over, so that when they go out on the highways, they can create their own rush hour. But I declined. Then on Thursday, after I had had the unsatisfactory visit with my former friends, Grandpa Izzy called with a different suggestion. He asked Dad to drop me off at their place in the morning before he went to work. Margaret's grandson Ethan, who was my age, had arrived, and Grandpa Izzy thought a visit would be good for both of us. I thought he meant Ethan and me, but maybe he meant Dad and me because after he took the call, the look on my father's face was a new way to spell relief.

My only requirement was that I be allowed to bring Ginger. A lot of retirement high-rises have rules against dogs, visiting or otherwise, and I did not know Margaret's position on dogs. Grandpa Izzy said that Ginger would not be a problem. Of course, she never was. Ginger is a genius.

I did not know if I was developing an interest in boys, or if I would have washed my hair and put on my new blouse anyway. Perhaps, I was leaving prepubescence and was entering full pubescence or, perhaps, I was simply curious about Ethan. For example, why had Margaret said nothing about his coming when we had seen each other at

Sunday's brunch? Margaret had mentioned having a grandson who was my age, but she said very little about him. Most grandmothers of her species carry a coffee-table-sized photo album in their tote-bag-sized pocketbooks. Either Margaret was a rare subspecies of grandmother or her grandson Ethan had done something strange to his hair. When grandmothers disapprove of grandsons, it is usually their hair. Their hair or their music. Or both. She must have known about his visit for at least two weeks because everybody I know has to buy airline tickets that far in advance to get the discount.

Grandpa Izzy's high-rise retirement condominium was three towns north of Dad's swinging singles apartment complex. The highway between them is bumper to bumper. Dad misjudged the time it would take to get there, so we did not arrive until after they had left for their morning walk. Dad gave me a key. I let myself in. There was a note on the refrigerator door saying that they had gone for their turtle walk and to make myself at home. The note was in Margaret's handwriting. No mistaking her *u*'s for *n*'s or her *i*'s for *e*'s. Margaret's handwriting was the smooth, round style used by the older generation of schoolteachers, which is exactly what Margaret was before she became an elementary school principal, which is what she was before she retired.

Ginger and I waited on the balcony and watched the three of them approach. Ethan appeared to be almost as tall as Margaret and almost as blond, but not for the same reason. From the distance of the balcony—it was the third floor—he appeared to be a healthy prepubescent. Of course, except for my father, appearances do not always tell much about a person's nervous condition.

The three of them were very excited when they returned.

Even though Ethan is Margaret's grandson, it was Grandpa who introduced me because Margaret did not. She went straight to the desk to dig a record book out of the drawer. "Ethan's lucky," Grandpa said. "Only his second day here, and this evening, we will be digging out one of our nests."

He was talking about turtle nests. Turtles had brought Grandpa and Margaret together.

The year after Bubbe Frieda had died, Grandpa Izzy sold their little house and moved to Century Village. For the next two years, early every morning, before the day got too hot, he drove to the beach where he took a walk. Many people from Century Village walked the beach where there was a sidewalk with markers for every half mile. A year ago last spring he noticed a blond zaftig woman who was returning about the same time he was leaving, so he began starting out earlier and earlier until, one day, they started out together. He introduced himself and asked her if she would like to take a walk with him. She replied by inviting him to join her on her turtle walk.

He accepted, not even knowing where or what it was.

And they had been doing it together ever since.

Margaret was checking in her record book. "We moved one hundred seven eggs," she said.

"We feel very protective of the nests we move," Grandpa explained to Ethan, who nodded as if he understood what Grandpa was talking about, leading me to believe that they had already explained turtles to him.

Sea turtles need beaches, of which Florida has many miles. All up and down the coastline, female turtles come out of the ocean and paddle their way across the sand, dig a hole, and lay eggs—about a hundred at a time. They use their flippers first to dig the hole and then to scoop the sand back over it before returning to the sea. The female will lay three to five clutches of eggs during a season, return to the water, and not come out of the water again for two or three years, when she is ready to lay again.

About fifty-five days after being laid, the eggs hatch.

From the first of May when the first eggs get laid until Halloween night when the last of them hatches, turtle patrols walk assigned stretches of beach. Members of a turtle patrol are trained to recognize the flipper marks that the mother turtles make.

About half the time the mother turtle lays her eggs in a dangerous place—where the eggs might get washed out because they are within the high tide line or where they might get trampled by people or run over by cars. Turtle eggs are a gourmet feast to birds, big fish, and especially raccoons. People approved by the Department of Environmental Protection are allowed to move the nests to safer ground. They post a stake with a sign over all the nests they find—the ones they move and the ones they do not—saying that it is against the law to disturb the nest. If you do, you can be fined up to $50,000 and/or go to jail for a year. The signs, which are bright yellow, make it very clear that it is an *and/or* situation.

Loggerheads are a threatened species. That means that they are not as seriously missing as endangered, but almost. Last year, encouraged by Grandpa Izzy, I did my science report on Florida turtles. We studied together. We accompanied Margaret on her turtle walks. (I called her Mrs. Draper then. I never guessed that only months later we would become almost related.) I got an A; Grandpa got permitted. Margaret had been permitted when they met.

I saved my report. I had begun it by asking, "Do you think it is harder to name Mr. Walter Disney's Seven Dwarfs or to name all five of the species of turtles that migrate off the coast of Florida?" My grandfather thought that was a wonderful way to begin a report. I had drawn a cover that showed all five kinds (loggerheads, greens, leatherbacks, hawksbill, and Kemp's ridley). My teacher commented on my cover, saying that it was exceptional. I saved the report because I thought I would draw a different cover—one showing a map of Florida beaches—and use it again in sixth grade when we were required to do a Florida history report. I did not know then that when I started sixth grade, I would be living in the state of divorce and New York.

Grandpa Izzy said, "Why don't you stay, Nadia? You've always enjoyed watching a nest being dug out. Ethan's coming." He looked over at Ethan, inviting him to reinforce the invitation. Ethan nodded slightly. "It'll be like old times," Grandpa said.

How could my Grandpa Izzy even begin to think that our digging out a nest would be like old times? In old times, which were not so very long ago, I would have enjoyed—even been excited about—digging out a turtle nest. In old times Margaret would still be Mrs. Draper, and I would neither know nor care that she had a grandson Ethan.

"When will this happen?" I asked.

"After sunset, as usual," Grandpa replied, looking at me curiously, for he knew I knew.

"Oh, that is too bad," I said. "Dad is picking me up before supper, and he will be disappointed if I do not eat with him."

Grandpa said that he would call Dad at work and have him stop over so that he, too, could watch. And before I could tell them the real truth—that I would rather not attend at all—they had Dad on the telephone and everything was arranged. I was not angry, but I was seriously annoyed.

That afternoon the four of us went to the pool. I had to leave Ginger back at the apartment because dogs were not allowed at poolside. I had not brought my bathing suit, so I had to sit by the pool while the others swam. Margaret said that she was sorry that she did not have a bathing suit to lend me. "I don't think mine will fit," she said. I think she was attempting to make a joke because she smiled when she said it.

I do not know who, besides Margaret herself, any bathing suit of hers would fit. She had what the catalogs call "a mature figure," and she was not at all self-conscious about it or the starbursts of tiny blue veins on both her inner and outer thighs. Bubbe Frieda had never been *zaftig*, but she had had the good taste to wear what is called "a dressmaker bathing suit." It had a little skirt and a built-in bra. Of course, my bubbe's bathing suit never got wet, and Margaret did forty-two laps.

Ethan practiced a few dives. Grandpa coached him. Then they came and sat by me. I was curious to know if Ethan's trip had been planned long before they announced it. I asked him if he had changed planes in Atlanta. He said that he had. "On my flight out of Atlanta, there were seven unaccompanied minors," I said.

He smiled. "There were only five on mine. I guess I was a little late in the season."

"Did you have an advance reservation?" I asked.

"Yes," he replied. "Why do you ask?"

"I was wondering," I said. I did not tell him what I was wondering about. "When you travel with a pet," I added, "you must plan in advance. The worst part of my trip was worrying about Ginger. She had to fly as baggage. We were advised to tranquilize her and put her in a dog carrier. Ginger had never been tranquilized before, and she has been dopey all week. She is just now getting back to her real self. I promised her that I will not do that again."

"How will you get her back?"

"I am going to talk to her and tell her to be quiet so that I do not have to tranquilize her."

"Maybe you just gave her too strong a dose."

"Maybe. But I do not care to experiment. She will make the trip fine. Ginger is a genius."

"Someone has written a book about the intelligence of animals. Border collies are smartest."

"Ginger would not be listed. She is a mixed breed. Like me."

"What's your mix?"

"Half-Jewish, half-Protestant."

"That's good," he said. "Like corn. It's called hybrid vigor."

I took that as a compliment, but I did not thank him for it. "Are you a hybrid?" I asked.

"Not at all. The only claim my family has to hybridization is right there," he said pointing to Margaret. "Grandma Draper is a thoroughbred Protestant, and Izzy is a thoroughbred Jew. But they don't plan on breeding."

I think I blushed.

Margaret was in charge of fifteen permitted volunteers. That meant that if she could not do the turtle patrol, one of them could. Permitted volunteers were licensed to move a nest or dig out a nest after the eggs had hatched, but they had to be supervised by her. All fifteen of Margaret's permitteds, plus friends and other interested parties showed up for the digging out. As soon as other beach walkers saw the hovering over the nest, they joined in. The audience was enthusiastic. They ooohed and aaahed, and at least once every three minutes, one way or another, someone said that nature was wonderful. Four people said, "Fascinating." Ethan did not oooh or aaah, and he did not say fascinating. He watched as patiently as a cameraman from *National Geographic*. My father hovered with the rest of them and said "fascinating" twice. Hovering had become his great recreational pastime.

Turtle patrols keep very close watch on all the nests on their stretches of beach, and they know when they are ripe for hatching, and sometimes they are lucky enough to be there when the turtle nests are emerging. That is what a hatching is called. When the turtles push their way out of the sand and start waddling towards the water's edge, they look like a bunch of wind-up toys escaped from Toys "R" Us. Watching a nest hatch is more interesting than digging one out after they've hatched, which is really only a matter of keeping inventory and making certain that everything that was or is living is cleared out. During old times, I had ooohed and aaahed at the digging out, but that evening it seemed as exciting as watching a red light change.

Like a proud parent, Margaret watched as Grandpa Izzy dug out the nest. Wearing a rubber glove on his hand, he reached down into the nest as far as his arm pit. He removed:

> 96 empty egg shells
> 4 unhatched whole eggs
> 1 dead hatchling
> 3 turtles that were half-in/half-out of the shell but were
>   dead. Those are called dead-pipped.
> 1 turtle that was half-in/half-out of the shell but was alive.
>   Those are called live-pipped.
> 2 live ones

Margaret took notes, counted again, and said at last that it all added up.

Grandpa released the two live turtles onto the sand. Everyone lined up on either side of them as they made their way to the water's edge.

Turtles almost always hatch at night, and after they do, they head toward the light. Normally, the light they head for is the horizon on the ocean. However, if a hotel or high-rise along the ocean leaves its lights on, the turtles will head toward the brighter light of civilization and never make it to the ocean. They do not find food, and they die. Turtles are not trainable animals. Their brains are in the range of mini to micro.

When the two hatchlings reached the water, everyone along the parade route applauded, and my father said fascinating for the third time.

Back at the nest, Margaret examined the live-pipped. She announced, "I've decided to keep it." Judge, jury, and defending attorney.

Dad asked what would happen to it, and Margaret explained, "It'll take a few days to straighten itself out. We'll give it a safe, cool, dark place in the utility room and release it after sunset when it's ready."

Dad could have asked me. I did get an A on that report.

When baby turtles come out of their shells, which are round—about the same size as a golf ball—they are squinched up into a round shape that fits inside the eggs. After they break through the shell, they spend three days down in the sand hole straightening themselves out.

Sometimes they die before they make it out of the shell. Those are the dead-pipped. They are counted and discarded with the unhatched and empties. A permitted person has to decide if the live-pipped are more alive than dead. If the decision is that they stand a good chance of surviving, they need care. They are lifted from the nest and taken home and given shelter until they straighten themselves out, and then they are released onto the sand.

"We never carry them to the water," Margaret explained. "They must walk across their native sand. We think that something registers in their brains that kicks in twenty-five years later because they return to the beach where they were born to lay their eggs."

As Margaret was explaining this, I thought about my mother's returning to New York. Her birthday is September 12, and I wondered if her need to return to autumn in New York had anything to do with some switch that had been turned on when she emerged.

Back at the condo, Grandpa carried the bucket containing the live-pipped into the utility room, and we all sat down to have milk and cookies. Oreos. Bubbe would have had homemade ruggelach. Margaret did not even know what ruggelach were until Grandpa Izzy took her to a kosher delicatessen and introduced her to them. She already knew about bagels because bagels have become popular even in places that never heard of them.

Margaret liked ruggelach, but I could tell she had no intention of learning how to make them. Grandpa Izzy, who had enjoyed ruggelach and bobka as much as anyone, had adjusted to Entenmann's and Oreos. I asked Ethan if he knew ruggelach. He did not. Knowing ruggelach is a hybrid advantage.

Before the evening was over, Grandpa Izzy suggested that Dad bring me back early enough so that I could take the morning turtle walk with him and Margaret and Ethan.

Then Margaret said, "Allen, why don't you come, too? The exercise will be good for your foot." Dad had broken his foot on the day of their wedding, and it had not yet healed. Margaret believed that a bad mental attitude had slowed it down. Much to my surprise, Dad agreed. "What about Ginger?" I asked.

"No problem," Grandpa Izzy said. "Just keep her on a leash like old times."

I started to say that Ginger has grown to hate the leash, but once again a look on Dad's face told me something, and I said nothing. So it was from a look of Dad's and a sentence left unspoken that the sequel to the turtle habit got started.

Dad and I would leave his apartment early, meet Margaret, Grandpa, and Ethan on the beach, and do our walk. Then Dad would return to Grandpa's and change into his business suit and leave for work. If time permitted, Dad would join us for breakfast. If not, the four of us would eat without him. We usually watched the rest of the *Today Show* before going for a swim.

Grandpa and Ethan got into an unofficial contest about how many laps they could do. I did not participate. I took a short swim, got out of the water, sat on the sidelines and read while Grandpa was teaching Ethan how to dive. He wanted to teach me, too, but I preferred not to.

One afternoon, we went to the movies. It was blazing hot and bright outside. We went into the movies where it was cool and dark, and then we came back out into the bright, hot sun. I felt as if I had sliced my afternoon into thirds, like a ribbon sandwich. Ethan, who never said much, had a lot to say about the camera angles and background music and described the star's performance as subtle. Never before in all my life had I heard a boy use the word subtle.

Dad had tickets for *The Phantom of the Opera.* This was the real Broadway show except that it was the road company. Not knowing that Ethan would be visiting, he had bought only four. As soon as he found out that Ethan would be in town, he started calling the ticket office to buy one more, but there were none to be had. He kindly volunteered to give up his ticket but Grandpa Izzy and Margaret would not hear of it. Margaret said that she would stay home, and Grandpa Izzy said that he didn't want to go if she didn't.

I expected Ethan to do the polite thing and say that he would stay home. But he did not. Of course, Ethan usually said nothing. Even when it was appropriate to say something, Ethan could be counted on to say nothing. But on the subject of who should give up a ticket, Ethan was particularly silent, which was a subtle hint that he really wanted to go. At the very last minute, the problem was solved. One of Dad's clients mentioned that he had an extra ticket, and Dad bought it from him on the spot.

We met at the theater. Ethan had insisted upon taking the odd seat, saying that he would be fine. The odd seat was three rows in front of ours and closer to the center of the stage, but I do not think Ethan knew it at the time. I think he wanted to be alone, or, I should say, without us. At intermission, Ethan bought one of the ten-dollar souvenir programs, and after the show he thanked my father at least five times for getting him a ticket.

Dad was pleased with the way the evening had turned out. We went to the Rascal House for ice-cream sundaes after the show. Ethan could hardly keep himself from thumbing through his ten-dollar program. His head must have stayed back at the theater long after we left, for when the waitress asked for his order, he said, "They must have more trapdoors on that stage than a magic act."

My father actually hummed as he looked over the menu, and then right after we placed our orders, he dropped his bombshell.

He asked Margaret if he could be listed on her permit. He would like to be able to substitute for her or Grandpa Izzy. His apartment house was not far from a beach, he explained, and he would transfer to someone's permit there after I went back north. Then he would like to train so that he could head up a turtle patrol. His goal was to get licensed.

"Like father, like son," he said, patting Grandpa Izzy on the back.

Margaret said, "We'll get the process started tomorrow." She must have been quite proud of her loggerheads. They got her my grandpa, and now they got her my dad.

I did not care. I had Ginger. I preferred animals with fur and some measure of intelligence. Ginger had grown sleek and muscular with our long turtle walks. She was more affectionate than ever. For example, when we got back to the apartment after *The Phantom of the Opera*, she greeted me as if I were the best friend she had ever had.

Inside me there was a lot of best friendship that no one but Ginger was using.

The day after Dad dropped his bombshell, he and Ethan, Margaret and Grandpa walked the beach together, a tight, three-generation foursome. They got ahead of Ginger and me, and I made no effort to catch up. Instead, I slowed down and walked at the water's edge so that I could kick at the waves as they rolled ashore. Ginger and I fell farther and farther behind the others. I saw Ethan stop to wait for

Ginger and me to catch up. He did not call to us, and I pretended that I did not notice. Ethan waited until Ginger and I were midway between Grandpa, Dad, and Margaret—until we were half-pipped—and then I slowed down even more. Dad stopped, called to Ethan—not to me—to catch up. Ethan looked toward Ginger and me, then toward Grandpa and Margaret, waited another second or two, and then walked fast-forward until he caught up with Dad, Grandpa, and Margaret.

On Tuesday evening we watched a nest hatch. It was one of theirs. "Theirs" means that it was one that Margaret had moved. Like the one on the first night of our turtle walks, this one also contained a hundred and seven eggs, but this time all one hundred seven turtles emerged. "One hundred percent," Grandpa cried, and he hugged Margaret. Then he congratulated Ethan and Dad. Ginger and I stayed on the fringe because I had to hold Ginger on a short leash so that she would not start chasing the baby turtles. Grandpa did not hug or congratulate me.

We all returned to Grandpa's apartment, and Dad insisted on taking us all out to the Dairy Queen to celebrate. Margaret ate a whole Peanut Buster Parfait without once mentioning cholesterol or calories.

I was sitting at poolside, reading. After doing our turtle walk, Margaret had gone to her volunteer duties at the garden club, and Grandpa Izzy had gone to his at the public library. Ethan and I were to let ourselves into their condo and start lunch. Ethan finished his laps and came out of the water. I joined him at the pool's edge and put my feet into the water, too. I noticed that he had his key on an elastic cord around his ankle, and I also noticed that he had a key chain ornament that looked like a giant molar. As the daughter of a dental hygienist, I was interested in his key chain ornament and asked where he got it.

"From your mother," he said.

I was not prepared for his answer. "My mother?" I asked in a voice that was too loud even for the out-of-doors.

"Well, yes. Your mother works for Dr. Gershom, doesn't she?"

"As a matter of fact, she does."

"She cleaned my teeth," he said.

There is not a worse feeling in this world than the feeling that someone knows something about you that he has known for almost a whole summer and has kept to himself. Even sharing what he knows about you with others is not as bad as knowing something and not telling you he knows. All you can think about is what he was really thinking the whole time he was speaking to you or walking the beach with you or swimming laps or playing fetch with your dog Ginger. I felt as if I had been spied on. I felt as if I had been stalked.

My heart was pumping gallons of blood up to my face. I could feel my neck throb. I controlled my voice so that it would not quiver. I said, "You should have told me that. You should have told me long before now. A person with good manners would have."

Ethan said, "I didn't think it was important."

I caught my breath and asked an intermediate question, "Does your mother also know Dr. Gershom?"

"He's our family dentist."

"And Margaret? Does she also know him?"

"I told you. He is our family dentist. Grandma Draper is part of our family. Before she moved to Florida, he was her dentist too."

"Do not adopt that tone with me, Ethan Potter."

"What tone?"

"The tone of being patient and tolerant as if the questions I am asking are dumb questions. They are not dumb questions. I need to know what you know that I do not."

"I don't know what you don't know, so how can I know what I know and you don't?"

"Now that is a dumb question. That is really a very stupid question."

"I don't think so."

"Just tell me what you knew about my mother and me and my father before we met."

"Okay. I'll tell you what I knew about you if you'll tell me what you knew about me."

"All right. You go first."

"When your mother said that she was divorcing your father and wanted to move to New York where she grew up, my grandmother set things up with Dr. Gershom."

"Margaret set what things up?"

"The job interview."

"Mother's job interview with Dr. Gershom?"

"I thought that was what we were talking about—your mother's job with Dr. Gershom."

"We are talking about what you know that I do not."

"And I am trying to tell you. Your mother told Izzy and Grandma Draper that she wanted to move to New York State, so Grandma set up a job interview with Dr. Gershom."

I had stayed in Florida with Dad while Mother had gone north to find a job and a house. No one—not Dad, not Mother, not Grandpa Izzy—no one had told me that Margaret had set up mother's job interview with Dr. Gershom. Margaret could have. The others should have. No one seemed to think that it should matter to me where I lived. No one seemed to think that it would matter to me whether I spent my life in New York or Florida or commuting between the two.

My throat was dry. I took a deep breath of the chlorine-saturated pool air and asked, "Is there anything else you know about me that I don't know?"

Ethan shrugged. "Only that Noah was best man at Grandma and Izzy's wedding."

"The whole world knows that. I am asking you one last time. What do you know about me that I do not know you know?"

"Not much. Only that Noah never said what nice guys your dad and Izzy are."

"That is what you do not know. I was asking you what you do know." The pulse in my neck was about to break through the skin.

"I do know that you're pretty mad right now, and I think now you ought to tell me what you knew about me."

"Nothing."

"My grandma told you nothing about me?"

"That is correct. She said nothing about you. She did not even tell me that you were coming even though she had several opportunities to do so."

Ethan then asked a strange question. "Did she tell you anything about Luke?"

"Luke what? Luke warm?"

"My brother Lucas, called Luke. Did she tell you anything about him?"

"She did not."

Ethan smiled, more to himself than to me. "Well," he said, "we Potters make an art of silence."

"Your grandmother is a Draper."

"See?" he said, grinning. "It comes to me from both sides of my family."

I did not speak to him for the rest of the day, and when he left the pool to return to the condo for lunch, I did not go with him. I thought that it would do him good to know how if felt to be the recipient rather then the giver of silence.

It was obvious that it was Margaret who had made possible my mother's leaving my father. Margaret Diamondstein, formerly Draper, helped my mother move to New York. She moved turtles from one nest to another. She moved Grandpa Izzy out of Century Village. And now, she was helping my father get permitted. By next turtle season, she will be helping him move to the beach. Margaret Diamondstein, formerly Draper, was an interfering person.

I did not need Margaret interfering with my life. I would have nothing more to do with her. That meant no more walking on the beach. That meant no more swimming and breakfast. That meant no more turtle walks.

Never again a turtle walk. Never.

I would stop and never tell her why.

Never.

I was still at the pool when Dad came to pick me up. I went back to the condo while they all went down to the beach to check on a nest. After I showered and dressed, I watched from the balcony, staying back by the wall where I could not be seen. Ginger whimpered to let me know that she wanted to be down there, but I thought that at the very least, my dog ought to stay by—and on—my side.

I wanted to leave my father's house. I wanted to go home, to autumn.

That evening as we were driving back to swinging singles, I asked my father if he knew that Margaret had set up Mother's job interview.

"I did."

"I think you could have told me."

"I didn't think it was important."

"Why does everyone think they know what is important to me? This was important. This *is* important. Do you think it is right that you should know and Ethan should know, and I should not?"

All he said was, "I didn't know that Ethan knew." I waited for Dad to say something more, to apologize, or simply tell me that I was right, but he did not. Like Ethan, my father has a strong taste for silence. Mother always said, "Your father is not a communicator." She made that statement more than once. Sometimes more than once a day. I was glad that I had made the decision not to go on any more turtle walks and not to communicate with anyone about my decision.

The following morning when Dad knocked on my door, I was still undressed. He called through the closed door, "Better hurry. We'll be late." I said nothing. He opened the door a crack and said, "Nadia? Nadia, are you all right?"

"I am not going," I said.

"What's the matter? Don't you feel well?"

"I feel fine. I have decided to stay here."

"Why?"

"It is not important."

Dad waited by the door, waited for me to explain, but I said nothing. I wanted silence to make him as miserable as it made me. He hesitated, then came into my room, sat on the edge of the bed, and said nothing. He hovered. I struggled with silence until I could not stand it another second, so I said, "Did you know that I did a report on turtles last year?"

"Yes. I knew that."

"You never seemed very interested in turtles when I did my report."

"I guess I had other things on my mind."

The pulse in my ears was so strong, I hardly heard him. "I guess it took an invitation from Margaret to get you interested."

"Partly that and partly that I had the time."

"Your child custody time," I said. Dad let out a long sigh and looked so embarrassed that I almost did not say what I was about to say, but I did. "I have decided not to spend your child custody time on turtle walks with Margaret and her grandson. Not today. Not tomorrow. Not ever. If you want to take turtle walks, you go ahead and take turtle walks. You can get permitted without me. All you need are turtles and Margaret." I had not only broken my silence, I was almost screaming.

Dad looked at his watch. If there is one thing I really detest, it is having someone look at his watch as he is talking to me. It says to me that time spent elsewhere is more important than time spent talking to me. "I have an appointment at the office in an hour." He glanced at his watch again.

"I am sure it is an important appointment," I said.

"Yes, it is," he replied.

Dad was so preoccupied with time that he did not even notice the sarcasm in my voice.

"Let me call Margaret to let her know we won't be there."

"You can go," I said. "You go. I would not want you to miss a turtle walk for my sake. It might interfere with your getting permitted."

"There's no way I can make it up there and back in time for my appointment."

"Are you trying to tell me that I have kept you from your turtle walk?"

"Well, no. But, yes." He looked confused. "What I meant to say is that, yes, this conversation has kept me from going on a turtle walk, but no, that is not what I am trying to tell you. You know that if it had not been for your unwillingness to go, I would have."

He glanced at his watch again. "Let me call Margaret. Then we'll have time for breakfast, and we'll talk about it." He started out the door, turned back and said, "I won't tell her why you're not coming."

"Tell her. I do not care. She knows every other thing about me. Tell her," I said. "And do not count on me for breakfast. I do not want any." I turned my back to him and my face to the pillow.

The telephone rang in the middle of the morning. I let the recorder get it. It was Margaret, telling me that she would come pick me up if I would call. I did not. Instead, I took Ginger for a walk around the golf course that borders swinging singles. When we returned, I saw that there was a message on the machine. I played it. It was Grandpa Izzy asking me to please call. I erased the message. I sat out by the pool for a while and read, came back to the apartment for lunch, and that is when I ate the breakfast cereal that my dad had put out on the counter in the kitchen. He called while I was eating. I did not pick the phone up then either.

After lunch, I took Ginger for another walk, called the airline to see how much it would cost if I changed my ticket to go home early. Thirty-five dollars. I watched three talk shows on television. One was about teenagers whose mothers flirt with their boyfriends. They were pathetic. Another was about men who said they lost their jobs because they refused to cut off their ponytails. They were pathetic. The third was about people who pierce weird body parts: One girl had a silver nail run through her bellybutton, and another one had a diamond stud put in her tongue. One exposed her bellybutton, and the other stuck out her tongue. They were disgusting. The phone rang twice. It was my dad, again sounding worried that I was not answering. Then it was Margaret again, saying that she hoped we would come over since another nest was due to hatch.

I erased all the messages.

Not answering the phone but hearing what people on the other end were saying was a little bit like spying. I enjoyed it.

Dad walked into the apartment looking frazzled. He was looking very much like the unstrung self who had picked me up from the airport. "Where were you?" he demanded. "I have been calling every twenty minutes."

"I noticed," I said. When he asked me why I had not returned his calls, I said that I did not think they were important.

"I'm taking tomorrow off," he said.

"What are you going to do?" I asked. "Hover?"

"What do you mean?"

"Nothing." *Nothing* is a mean answer, but sometimes nothing works. Sometimes nothing else does.

"I thought we might go up to Disney World. You used to like Epcot."

"What will I do with Ginger?" I asked.

"Well, let me find out what accommodations they have for dogs. . . ."

Just then the phone rang. Dad picked it up. I could tell by the way he was speaking that it was Grandpa Izzy asking if he would be coming for the evening's turtle walk. When he hung up, Dad asked me if I would like to invite Ethan to come to Disney World with us. I could not believe he was asking me that question. I just stared at him.

"Well," he said, "he seemed to enjoy *The Phantom of the Opera* so much, I thought he might enjoy . . ." I continued to stare at my father and say nothing. He cleared his throat. "If you don't like the idea of asking Ethan, would you like to ask one of your friends from the old neighborhood?" He was practically pleading with me to ask someone. Without turtles my father did not know what to do with me.

Even though Disney World was only a two hours' drive from his apartment, Dad had decided that it might be more fun if we stayed overnight at one of Disney's theme hotels. He called and got us reservations, and we went to our rooms to pack our overnight bags.

That evening a northeaster hit the coast. The winds were thirty-five miles an hour with gales up to fifty. There was coastal flooding, which meant that the low lying highways and many side roads and ramps would be closed. That meant that the interstates that were normally bumper to bumper but moving would be bumper to bumper and not moving. Before we went to bed, Dad suggested that we avoid rush hour by starting out late in the morning instead of early.

The phone rang at midnight. Dad called in to me and said that I should pick up the phone. It was Grandpa Izzy.

"It's an emergency," he said, pleading. "Our hatchlings will be swept ashore by the winds. We have to harvest them early tomorrow before daylight. Before the birds get them. Margaret and I think you ought to drive up here now so that we can get an early start. Traffic will be impossible in the morning."

Grandpa was so sincere, so concerned about the turtles, so convinced that we would answer his 911 that it was obvious Dad had never told him that I had canceled all future turtle walks. I waited to see how Dad would turn him down. Dad did his best thing, he remained silent.

Grandpa said, "Nadia, are you there? Are you on the line, darling?"

"I am here, Grandpa. . . ."

"You know what will happen if we don't gather them up. Can't you come?"

"Dad and I had plans . . ."

"What plans, darling? You don't want the baby turtles to be blown ashore and die, do you? These are babies, Nadia. They need help."

"Dad and I were going to Epcot . . ."

"Why do you want to go there to see Mr. Walter Disney's Version of the World when you can see Mother Nature's real thing?" I had to smile. Grandpa Izzy always called Disney World *Mr. Walter Disney's Version of the World*. Then he said, "Margaret and I need your help, Nadia. So do the turtles. Sometimes one species has to help another get settled." Grandpa was apologizing for not telling me about Margaret's meddling. I did not know what to say.

Dad finally spoke up, "Let Mother Nature worry about the turtles. They can take care of themselves."

But I knew that they could not. I said, "Let me talk to Dad, Grandpa. I will call you back."

After I hung up, I went into the living room. Dad was in his pajamas. Striped. I had never seen Dad sitting in the living room in striped pajamas. He said, "Don't worry about the turtles, Nadia."

I explained, "The turtles will be easy to spot—so out of place, washed up on the shore. The birds will eat them."

"They couldn't possibly eat them all."

"Those that do not get eaten will be lost."

"But, surely, the tide will come back and carry the seaweed—and the turtles along with it—back out." He smiled again. "What comes ashore always washes back out. That's not a philosophical statement, Nadia. It's a fact."

"They will be lost at sea."

"Lost at sea? The sea is their home."

"They will be lost at sea," I repeated.

"Nadia," Dad said, "how can that happen?"

"You have to understand turtles to understand how that will happen."

"I don't think I do."

"I told Grandpa I would talk to you."

My father sat on the sofa, looking out of place in his striped pajamas. He nodded, a slow, thoughtful nod, and I knew that he would pay close attention, and I knew that I could explain it all.

"It all starts," I said, "the minute the new hatchlings scamper over the sand toward the light of the horizon. Once they reach the water, they begin a swimming frenzy. They do not eat. They just swim and swim until they reach the Sargasso Sea. That is when they stop, and that is when Mother Nature turns off the swimming-frenzy switch and turns on a graze-and-grow switch. For the next five to ten years, they will stay in the Sargasso Sea, feeding off the small sea animals that live in floating mats of sargasso grass. Tonight when the wind blows that seaweed ashore, there will be a lot of immature turtles in it—swept along with the sea grass they have called home."

I paused in my narrative. I focused hard on Dad, and he focused hard on me. "Are you with me?" I asked. My father nodded, so I continued. "Here is the tragic part. Even if the tide does wash them back into the water, they will not be able to get back home because once the swimming-frenzy switch is turned off, it is turned off forever. Turtles do not have an emergency power pack or a safety switch to turn it on. So, there they are, once again at the water's edge, but this time they are without a mechanism for swimming east. And that is why they will be lost at sea. They will want to graze. They will have an appetite, but they will not be where they can satisfy it, and they will not know how to get there because they cannot turn back their internal clock. They will not find home. They will not find food. They will starve and grow weak and be eaten."

My father did not once look at his watch or the clock on the table by the sofa. His listen-and-learn switch had been turned on, and his own internal clock was ticking. I studied my father, sitting on the pale gray living room sofa in his blue striped pajamas. The storm in our private lives had picked him up and put him out of place. Me, too. I, too, had been picked up from one place and set down in another. I, too, had been stranded. We both needed help resettling.

"When Grandpa says that we must harvest the turtles, he means that we must gather them up and save them in buckets. Then we take them to Marineland. When the seas calm down, they will be taken fifty miles offshore and placed in the Sargasso Sea."

Dad smiled. "They need a lift."

Ginger rubbed herself against my legs. I stroked her back. "Yes," I said, "they do."

Without another word, we returned to our rooms, Dad and I. We got dressed. When we ran out to the car, the rain was coming down in sheets, and the wind was blowing so hard that umbrellas were useless. I held the back door open for Ginger, and she hopped in. Dad and I got pretty wet just from that short run to the car, and Ginger sat on the back seat, panting and smelling like the great wet dog she was.

The rain battered the car, and the wipers danced back and forth, never really clearing the windshield. There were only a few cars on the road. We didn't pass any of them not only because it was danger-ous to do so but also because we welcomed their red tail lights as a guide. Cars coming the other way made spray that splashed over the hood. Dad's hands were clenched on the steering wheel.

These northeasters dump rain in squalls that last for miles, and then they let up briefly. During one of the few lulls in the storm, Dad leaned back slightly and asked, "What do the turtles do after they've finished their five to ten years in the Sargasso Sea?"

"They go to the Azores and become bottom feeders for a few years."

"And then?"

"And then they grow up. When they are about twenty-five, they mate. The females come ashore and lay their eggs—on the same shore where they were born—and immediately return to the sea, not coming ashore again for two or maybe three years when they are again ready to lay eggs. The males never return to shore."

Dad said, "You've left something out, Nadia. They are ten when they leave the Sargasso Sea, and they are twenty-five when they mate and lay eggs. What happens during the fifteen years between leaving the Azores and mating?"

Realization hit me. I laughed out loud. We were riding into a squall again, and Dad was concentrating so hard on driving that I was not sure he was even waiting for my answer. "What is it?" he asked.

"Another switch," I asked.

He took his eyes off the road long enough to demand, "Tell me, what do they do?"

"In the years between leaving their second home and their return to their native beaches, they commute. Year after year, all up and down the Atlantic, turtles swim north in the summer and south in the winter. Did you already know that?"

"I didn't know for sure, but I had my suspicions."

I had to smile. "And did you have your suspicions about me?"

"For a while," he said. Then he took his eyes off the road long enough to return my smile. "But not now."

"Of course," I said, "I will be doing the same but opposite. I will commute north in the winter and south in the summer."

"Yep," he said. "And there will be times when you or I will need a lift between switches."

"Yes," I replied, "there will be times."

Three

Mrs. OLINSKI'S very first teaching job had been in an elementary school whose principal required sixth graders to memorize at least fourteen lines of poetry each month, insisted that fifth graders know their multiplication tables up through twelve times twelve, and permitted no one to exchange valentines unless the names on the envelopes were written neatly and spelled correctly. There was no graffiti on the walls; no gum chewing, running, or shoving in the halls. There was locker inspection once a month, and everyone who used the bathroom, flushed.

That principal's name was Margaret Draper.

Two years before Margaret Draper retired, the district reorganized its school system and sent sixth graders to middle school instead of elementary. Sixth had once been the top grade in elementary school, and was now the bottom grade in middle school. But it was still the place where kids had mastered enough skills to be able to do something with them. It was still the place where kids could add, subtract, multiply and divide, and read. Mostly, they could read—really read. Sixth grade still meant that kids could begin to get inside the print and to the meaning.

Mrs. Margaret Draper, who had never called herself an ed-you-kay-toar, had always been a superb teacher and principal, but between the time she had started as an elementary school teacher and the time she had retired as a middle school principal, sixth grade had changed, but sixth graders had changed more. Sixth graders had stopped asking "Now what?" and had started asking "So what?" She had not been sorry to retire when she did.

That very first summer after Margaret Draper retired was when Eva Marie Olinski left teaching. That was the summer of her automobile accident. For all the many months following the accident, Mrs. Draper stayed in touch with the young Mrs. Olinski. They were both widows now, and they saw each other on a regular basis.

After Margaret moved to Florida they continued to stay in touch in a Christmas card/life-milestone way. So Mrs. Olinski knew the major facts of Margy's life. Her move to Century Village, her marriage to Izzy Diamondstein, her trips, her turtles.

Mrs. Olinski also knew that Ethan Potter was Margaret Draper's grandson even though Margy never had much to say about him. When Eva Marie saw that Ethan Potter was assigned to her homeroom, she refrained from asking Margy about him or Ethan about her. She wanted to discover Ethan all by herself, so she watched him closely. Probably more closely than she watched the others.

Ethan was smart, yes; he had a certain independence of mind, yes, and he still asked "Now what?" instead of "So what?"

When Mrs. Olinski decided that Ethan should be a member of her team, she did not tell Margy or, for that matter, anyone else either.

* * *

The commissioner of education of the state of New York smiled as he read the next question. "The following places in New York State are associated with women famous in American history. I shall name the place; you are required to tell me why it is important and name the woman associated with that place. You may choose three of the four places. If you answer all four, you will receive an extra two-point credit. If you chose to answer only three, the other team will have an opportunity to answer the fourth, and if correct, will receive one point.

"The place names are: Seneca Falls, Homer, Rochester, and Auburn."

Ethan rang in as the last syllable sounded.

Yes.

Ethan Potter would know all four parts.

Yes, yes, yes, and yes.

Ethan Explains the B and B Inn

I am always the longest rider. I live farther from school than anyone else on my route. I board the bus first and get off last. I always have. The bus ride is the worst part of the school day. It always has been. Going is bad; coming home is worse.

On the first day of the new school year, I boarded the bus as usual, nodded to Mrs. Korshak, the driver, and walked to the back of the bus. All the way to the back. It was an unwritten rule that the seat you chose the first day became your assignment—unless you were so unruly that Mrs. Korshak made you change. I chose the last double seat on the side opposite the driver. I placed my backpack on the seat next to me, and as nonchalantly as I could, placed my leg over that. If luck held—as it had for the past two years—when the other kids boarded, they would choose seats that appeared to be less occupied, and I would not have to share my seat for the rest of the school year.

I knew every stop along the route. I knew every house, every tree and shrub, every pothole in the road. My father is proud of the fact that there have been Potters in Clarion County since before Epiphany was a town.

There is a fuzzy, faded picture of my great-great-great-grandmother in the Clarion County Museum. The museum is located in the main room of an old schoolhouse that the local historical society saved from the wrecker's ball by having it declared an historical landmark. My ancestor is marching behind Susan B. Anthony who is leading a group to the polls in Rochester. In the picture, my ancestor is wearing bloomers, which was what they called the trousers that were invented by Amelia Jenks Bloomer of Homer, New York, and suffragette is what they called the women who were fighting for a woman's right to vote. Instead of getting to vote, my triple-great-grandmother got arrested.

There is no picture of her at the first convention for women's rights, but she was there. In the family archive, which my Grandmother Draper passed on to my mother when she moved to Florida, there is a letter from her, postmarked Seneca Falls and dated 1848.

There have been farmers and educators on both sides of my family ever since there have been tractors and blackboards, and there have been strong women on my mother's side for just as long.

Last August when I was visiting my grandmother Draper in Florida, notice came that my homeroom teacher for grade six would be Mrs. Olinski. Unless she proved to be someone who had changed her name because of marriage or some other legal procedure, she would be new to Epiphany Middle School. I hoped she was. Having a teacher who didn't know I had an older brother would be a welcome change.

There is nothing wrong with Lucas, and that is what is wrong with him. He is a genius, a star athlete, and is always doing something wonderful and/or record setting. Half the population of Epiphany is convinced that Luke Potter will become so famous that his name will become a noun like Kleenex or Coke. The other half is convinced that Luke Potter will become a verb like Xerox or fax. And if someday, someone says, "*Luke* me that information, please," that information will be organized, memorized, and set to music.

Luke is six years older than I. He is in college now, but that has not put an end to his reputation. He has become a myth like Paul Bunyan or Davy Crockett. Because my name is Potter but not Lucas, I have been a disappointment to every one of my teachers during my previous six years—kindergarten counts.

The bus swung through the winding streets of The Farm, the subdivision that was made out of the Sillington place. The last of the Sillington sisters died and left their land to Clarion College. The college didn't want a farm, so it sold all the surrounding land to a developer who put in roads, sidewalks, and sewers, divided it up into lots, and sold it to builders. Every subdivision has a name. They named this one The Farm. It is no more a farm than the Aquarium at Epcot is the Atlantic.

None of the historical residents of Epiphany liked the idea of having the Sillington place parceled off for a subdivision. My parents, for example, hated it. My mother says that if people want to live in a place where every tree and shrub is put in place by a landscape architect, why don't they go live in a theme park? Mother avoids the subdivision as if it were a toxic waste dump. She refers to the people who live in The Farm as *them*. In her mind, there is a big difference between *them* and *us*, between living *on* a farm and living *in* The Farm. To *them* farming is a lifestyle not a livelihood. The fact that milk comes from cows has probably occurred to *them*, but *they* prefer to think of it as recycled grass.

The way I see it, the difference between farmers and suburbanites is the difference in the way we feel about dirt. To *them*, the earth is something to be respected and preserved, but dirt gets no respect. A farmer likes dirt. Suburbanites like to get rid of it. Dirt is the working layer of earth, and dealing with dirt is as much a part of farm life as dealing with manure: Neither is user-friendly but both are necessary.

When the bus picked up the last passengers from the last stop in The Farm, I lifted my leg off my backpack. My foot had fallen asleep, and it felt heavy as I lowered it. I rested it on the floor and allowed the pinpricks of blood to tease their way back up my leg. I shook my leg a little—not wanting to draw attention to myself—and turned my back to the aisle and gazed out the window. I am very good at gazing. I am also very good at listening. Gazing and listening are all right for church, but they sure kill a lot of conversations.

Instead of making its way back to the state road that parallels the lake, the bus took a left turn and started down Gramercy Road, the road that borders The Farm and the last within the two-mile radius that allows free bus transportation. Was I the only one who noticed that the bus was making an unscheduled stop? The only house there is the Sillington place. No one lives there. The house, which was given to the college along with the farm, was in a state of disrepair, and the college wanted to tear it down, but since it was the oldest farmhouse in Clarion County, it was saved by the same group that saved the schoolhouse. It is a huge old farmhouse that has had so many add-ons it looks like a cluster of second thoughts. About a hundred years ago, someone added a wraparound porch with enough gingerbread trim to look like a lace collar. The main feature of the first floor is the dining room, which stretches from the front of the house to the back because in the days when the Sillington place was a working farm, Mrs. Sillington used to feed all the itinerant farmhands breakfast and supper. They ate at long trestle tables that stretched the length of the room. There is a picture in the museum. When the Sillingtons first settled in Clarion County, before there was a state road parallel to the lake, they owned all the land down to the water's edge. The house itself is perched atop a knoll, and from the upstairs windows you get a good view of the lake.

I continued to stare out the window as the bus rolled down Gramercy Road. The Sillington house came into view. Standing at the edge of the drive was a man and a kid. The man was wearing a long navy blue apron and a white turban. A turban. A white turban. Like an illustration from *The Arabian Nights*. Equally strange: The kid was wearing shorts and knee socks. No one in Epiphany wears shorts on the first day of school. Even if it is ninety-five degrees in the shade—and sometimes it is—no one wears shorts on the first day of school. And no one—ever—wears knee socks with shorts. No one. Ever.

The kid was holding a leather book bag. Ever since backpacks were invented, no one—ever—in the entire school system, grades K through twelve, carries a book bag, especially a leather one.

The kid boarded the bus, the dark man wearing the long apron waved, and the kid stopped at the top of the steps and waved back. Even first graders on the first day of school don't do that.

The kid started making his way to the back of the bus. Before I could resume my seat-occupied sprawl, the kid was standing in the aisle next to my seat.

"Is this seat occupied?" he asked.

No one ever asks. They just stand in the aisle until you move and make room for them. Even if he had asked if the seat was *taken* instead of asking if it was *occupied*, I could have told that he had a British accent. He didn't look British. His skin was the color of strong coffee with skim milk—not cream—added; the undertones were decidedly gray. His lips were the color of a day-old bruise. He had more hair than you would think a single skull could hold. His hair—blue-black, thick and straight—did not have the hard sheen of the hair of a Chinese or Japanese but had the soft look of fabric.

"Julian Singh," he said, extending his hand. No one (a) introduces himself and then (b) extends his hand to be shaken while (c) wearing shorts and (d) knee socks and (e) holding a genuine leather book bag on (f) the first day of school.

I extended my hand. "Ethan Potter," I said. I did not smile. How could I? For a single moment of neglect, I would be stuck with having this kid as a bus partner for the rest of the school year.

I didn't want to set up any expectations. I wanted to ignore Julian Singh for the rest of the ride, and I managed to say nothing until the bus had turned left off Gramercy and was back on Highway 32, but then curiosity got the best of me. "Did you buy the Sillington house?" I asked.

"Yes," Julian replied. "The purchase was completed several weeks ago. There were quite a few delays in arranging the permits."

"Permits?" I asked

"Yes. Permits. Father is converting Sillington House into a B and B."

"A B *and B?*"

"Yes. A bed and breakfast inn. Rather like a small hotel. Except we will not be responsible for dinners, and thus we will support only a limited menu. Actually, the kitchen in Sillington House is quite remarkable. It is as large as many full-service restaurant kitchens. We must make Sillington House handicap accessible before we are ready for occupancy. Mrs. Gershom was most helpful in getting permits for the conversion."

"I'll bet she was," I said. "Is your father a cook?"

"Yes." Julian smiled. "A chef. He was chef on board the *Skylark*, the cruise ship. Father decided that we needed to settle down. He has always wanted to own an inn, so he purchased Sillington House. That is what we will call it."

"That is what it has always been called."

"Yes. So Mrs. Gershom informed us. Father believes that with the college nearby, many visiting parents will welcome such a place."

"Indeed," I said. I don't think I ever said that word before. What is there about an English accent that makes people seem more intelligent than they maybe are? And was it catchy?

I turned to the window and rested my forehead against the pane. How did he come by his English accent? Where did he go to school before? Was he really unaware of being weird? How did he get to be so weird? But enough was enough. If I didn't pocket my curiosity, I would be giving away more than a bus seat.

When the bus stopped, in a feeble attempt to postpone the inevitable, I pretended to be looking for something. Mrs. Korshak waited, watching in her rearview mirror. At last after everyone else had left, I walked the length of the aisle and stood for a second at the top of the steps.

There was Julian Singh waiting for me.

I knew he would be.

Julian said, "I am assigned to Mrs. Olinski, Room Twelve. Are you nearby?"

"I guess so," I replied, holding up my room assignment notice.

"What a stroke of luck," Julian said.

"Indeed," I replied.

Mrs. Olinski was the first teacher Epiphany ever had who taught from a wheelchair.

She sat, waiting, until we were all seated. Then she introduced herself. "I am Mrs. Olinski. I am one of those people who gets to use all those good parking spaces at the mall." She turned toward the blackboard and wrote in big block letters:

MRS. OLINSKI
PARAPLEGIC

As she wrote *paraplegic*, Mrs. Olinski spelled it out, "P-A-R-A-P-L-E-G-I-C. It means that I am paralyzed from the waist down." Her voice was steady, but I noticed that her hands were not. The O of Olinski was not round or smooth but nervous. I don't know what made me look at Julian Singh at that moment, but I did. He sat upright in his chair, not looking at Mrs. Olinski or the blackboard but staring into the middle distance, as if looking at the word *paraplegic* or the paraplegic herself was too painful.

Mrs. Olinski told us that she had become paralyzed in an automobile accident. Confined to a wheelchair as she was, she could not reach the top portion of the blackboard, so, stretch though she would, the words were written in the middle of the board—eye level for most standing sixth graders.

Hamilton Knapp, who had taken a seat in the very last row, farthest from the door, stood up and said, "Excuse me, Mrs. Olinski, but I can't see what you've written. Could you write a little higher on the blackboard, please?"

Mrs. Olinski smiled. "Not at the moment," she said.

Ham sat down and said, "Sorry." She didn't mean that smile, and Ham Knapp didn't mean that "sorry."

The remainder of the morning was taken up with bookkeeping matters such as passing out supplies and assigning seats. We were seated in alphabetical order, and as luck would have it, Ham Knapp ended up way back in the room, in the very seat he had chosen for himself.

Nadia Diamondstein was seated three rows over and two rows forward. I could see her red hair. Nadia and I were almost related. This past summer, her grandfather had married my grandmother. In August when I visited them, Nadia was visiting her father. We often walked the beach together. And one day after a storm, we rescued a batch of hatchling turtles and took them out to sea.

The light from the window shone on Nadia's side of the room. When she moved her head, the morning light caught in her hair the way the sun had when she turned her back to the ocean. Fringes of her hair framed her face in a halo. Whenever that halo effect happened, I wanted to stare at her until the sunlight stopped, but my heart stopped before the light did. Then there was a period during my vacation when Nadia chose not to walk with her father and me. I waited for her to catch up, and when I did, she slowed down, and I missed seeing the light in her hair. I never told Nadia how much I liked seeing the halo the sunlight made of her hair. Sometimes silence is a habit that hurts.

Noah Gershom sat in back of Michael Froelich and in front of Hamilton Knapp. His father is our family dentist. His mother sells houses—a lot of them in The Farm—and for reasons too complicated to tell, Noah Gershom was best man at my grandmother Draper's wedding early last summer. It was pretty funny the way it happened, but my mother, who was maid of honor, was not amused. She cannot forgive Mrs. Gershom for selling houses at The Farm. I think she would change dentists if there were another one as good in Epiphany. Potters have always taken good care of their land and their teeth.

Julian Singh sat in the row to my right and two seats back.

At lunchtime, I sat on the end of the bench. Noah took a seat next to me. Nadia came from the food line carrying her tray and found no vacant seat at any of the girls' tables so she sat next to Noah. Julian, who had brought his lunch, was seated at a table at the far end of the room, all alone. He finished eating and left the cafeteria without waiting for the bell or asking permission. When Mrs. Olinski saw him leave, she followed. She must have wanted to tell him the rules without calling him out to embarrass him. It took her a while to maneuver her wheelchair between the tables, so Julian had a head start. Shortly after Mrs. Olinski made her way through the door, the bell did ring, and we all left, and were just behind Mrs. Olinski as she made her way down the hall.

When we entered the classroom, we saw that someone had erased PARAPLEGIC and written CRIPPLE instead. Julian was the only person in the room. He was facing the blackboard, holding an eraser. He turned around, looking startled when he saw us file in, led by Mrs. Olinski in her wheelchair.

Mrs. Olinski approached him wordlessly. She held out her hand, and Julian silently handed over the eraser. Mrs. Olinski turned from him to the blackboard and slowly and deliberately erased the word CRIPPLE.

The question was: Had Julian erased PARAPLEGIC, or was he in the process of erasing CRIPPLE? I glanced back at Hamilton Knapp and saw him exchange a look and a slight smile with Michael Froelich, and I knew the answer.

Julian Singh quickly took the trophy for being the strangest person to ride the bus. It took only two days for the other kids to make his life miserable. They stuck their feet into the aisle of the bus to trip him as he made his way toward the back, but even though he seemed to have his eyes focused straight ahead, he managed to stop just short of protruding feet and say in his perfect British accent, "Beg your pardon. Would you mind?" And he would patiently wait in the aisle until they pulled their legs in. They had to pull their legs in because Mrs. Korshak would not start the bus rolling until everyone was seated. When they tried again, they met the same result. Again. The same.

No normal person would continue to be cheerful and wear short pants.

I knew what they would do next. And sure as God made green apples, they did.

Their next form of torment was to repeat whatever Julian said in an exaggerated imitation of his accent. They tossed *I say* and *beg your pahdon* front to back and across the aisle. Julian knew that he was the butt of their jokes, and I could tell that he cared, for I could see his cheeks glow red. But he said nothing, and kept his distance, or whatever distance he could manage on a crowded bus.

I still looked out the window during the ride to and from school and never spoke beyond answering "Hi" to his cheerful "Good morning." I always managed to delay getting off the bus long enough so that I would be last. I stood at the top of the stairs long enough to irritate Mrs. Korshak. It took a full week before Julian took the hint that I did not choose to walk with him from the bus to the building.

About the third day that Julian started off for class without waiting for me, I stood at the top of the stairs of the bus, checking to see if he was gone and spotted Michael Froelich waiting just inside the schoolyard fence by the side of the gate where we entered. As soon as Julian was clear of the other kids, I saw Froelich get into a crouch and I knew what was coming.

I ran down the bus steps and hooked my arm through Julian's and began walking rapidly toward school. Julian hardly had time to react before we were at the gate. I held onto Julian, blocking him from Michael Froelich.

From the foot of the schoolhouse stairs, Hamilton Knapp came barreling toward us. He grabbed Julian's book bag and ran with it to a tree beyond the school fence. My saving him from Froelich had slowed his chasing Knapp. He disentangled his arm and started toward Ham, but now his way was blocked by Michael, running backward, waving his arms like a guard in a game of basketball.

Julian didn't call for help. He didn't call out at all. Not even with a begging look in his eyes did he ask for help. Julian, who proved to be stronger and quicker than I would have guessed, escaped, ran to Ham, and managed to retrieve his book bag after a serious tug-of-war, but not before Ham Knapp had managed to write "I am a ass" with a black felt tip pen.

No one said anything about the incident. During the day, Julian put his book bag with the written side against the wall of his cubby, and on the way home that evening, he kept the written side of his book bag against his leg. I knew that the pen Ham used would leave permanent marks on leather.

The following morning Julian waited at the bus stop, still wearing short pants and knee socks. It was really the knee socks that did it. Short pants, tube socks, and Reeboks would have been a little off-center but not weird. He boarded the bus, waved to his father, and said "Good morning" as he took his seat.

Between *a* and *ass*, he had squeezed in a *p*. And in the space beneath that, he had changed the message. His book bag now read:

I am a passenger
on Spaceship Earth

A lightened ring in the leather around the first four syllables where someone had made several attempts to erase the writing looked like a halo.

I admired that halo. I guess I like halos.

Following the book bag incident, things on the bus cooled down, and so did the weather. Julian began to wear long pants—corduroys. I wondered if he even owned a pair of jeans.

The time of year had come when the after-school hours were growing shorter and shorter, and I had pumpkins to attend to. Every Saturday morning from June until mid-November, I went with

Mother to the Farmers' Market and helped her sell her fresh produce and free range eggs. In September and October we sold a lot of pumpkins. Mother paid me, and I saved almost all of it.

I was the son who was scheduled to inherit the farm because Luke was scheduled for greater things. I knew that as soon as I announced to my family what I wanted to do, I would have to be prepared to pay my own way.

There was no one in Epiphany to whom I could tell my plans. No one in Epiphany would believe that Ethan Potter wanted to go to New York City to work in the theater. I didn't want to be an actor. I wanted to design costumes or stage sets, but I could not tell anyone. In mental mileage, Epiphany, New York, is farther from New York City, New York, than the road mileage from New York to Hollywood.

Last summer Nadia Diamondstein's father took us to see *The Phantom of the Opera*. I had seen high school plays and plays that Clarion U. had put on, but I had never seen something like that. When that chandelier came down from the ceiling, my throat went dry. No one I knew was sitting by me, and I squeezed the arms of my chair to keep myself from getting up to cheer. I had seen football fans act the way I felt. I dream about that show. I bought a souvenir booklet that cost ten dollars, and I had looked at it so often that I was wearing the gloss off its pages. Someday I'm going to design costumes for a show like that.

But first I had to harvest pumpkins.

On the third Saturday after school began, Julian and his father appeared at market. I saw them first from a distance. They did not stand out in that crowd because the Clarion County Farmers' Market attracts a lot of people from the college, and the college in turn attracts a lot of dark-skinned people. Julian's father was carrying a basket over his arm. A lot of the college people and suburbanites believe it is the ecological thing to do. I saw Julian pointing me out to his father before they made their way to our booth.

Julian introduced his father to both Mother and me. Mr. Singh sang the praises of the quality of the goods at the market. (Everyone does. There is a rule that you cannot sell anything at the market that you do not grow or make yourself.) He said that as soon as his B and B opened for business, he would become a regular customer.

When they left, Mother asked about them. She had never before expressed a friendly interest in the fate of the Sillington house. I told her as much as I knew.

On the following Saturday, Julian and his father came to our booth again. Mr. Singh took forever to select four pumpkins from the $2.50 pile. They were not very big, but they were so similar in shape and size that they looked like clones. Julian handed me a ten dollar bill. I hated that. I don't know why I hate taking money from someone my age even though it isn't charity. I took the money, which was folded in half, and said, "Thank you." A lot of the booth operators say, "Have a nice day." I never do. Mother never does either. Sometimes she'll say, "Enjoy," but never "Have a nice day." Except for Uncle Lew who was in politics, Potters are famous for not saying anything they don't mean.

I waited until Julian and his father were on the far side of the next booth before I unfolded the ten-dollar bill. A small Post-it note was attached inside the fold. I glanced at it, couldn't understand it, looked at it harder, and decided to pocket the money with the note instead of putting it in the cashbox. I'd make it up with Mother.

Business was brisk the entire morning, and that was good. It meant that there would be fewer pumpkins to reload. I didn't have a chance to give Julian's note a second glance or a second thought. Well, maybe I did give it a second thought but not a third and not for long.

At home I waited until I was alone in my room before taking the ten-dollar bill from my pocket. I peeled the Post-it from inside the fold.

Alice's Adventures in Wonderland
Chapter VII Title

I found the book on the shelf in the living room and carried it upstairs. I closed my bedroom door, sat on the edge of my bed, and turned the pages until I came to Chapter VII, the chapter called "A Mad Tea Party."

This was obviously an invitation. The strangest I had ever received. I not only had never been invited to a tea party before but had never before been invited to a party where I was not told the time and place. Either the mystery would clear up, or it wouldn't. Either way, I wouldn't give it a second thought or discuss it with anyone.

Including Julian Singh.

Having established my habit of not speaking to Julian on the bus, it was easy to avoid talking about the message in the ten-dollar bill. And, to his credit, Julian gave no hint—no secret smiles or glances out of the corner of his eye—to indicate that he was waiting for a response. Instead, he boarded the bus, walked to the back, said "Good morning" just as he always did and said nothing for the rest of the way. And he did not wait for me at the foot of the bus steps.

I once again managed to be the last one off the bus. As I picked up my backpack, I found a Post-it note attached to the underside of the left shoulder strap. I pulled it off and read it.

> *Tea Time is always* 4:00 P.M.
> *World Atlas*
> *Map 4: D–16*

I put it in my shirt pocket.

Our class would be in the school media center after lunch. We were allowed to browse for the first fifteen minutes. I found the atlas. Map 4 was New York State. D-16 of Map 4 was Clarion County. On the page facing Map 4 was a drawing of a house with a lacy wrap-around porch. The address, 9424 Gramercy Road, was written beneath it. I took the drawing from the book and put it in my shirt pocket with the other two notes. I now knew the what, the where, and part of the when. I still didn't know the date.

As I returned to my study table, I passed Nadia Diamondstein among the stacks. She was in the fiction section, removing a book from the D's. *D for Dodgson,* Lewis Carroll's real name. I watched Nadia quickly leaf through the book she held in her hand, then go check it out. It was *Alice's Adventures in Wonderland.*

That evening as I was undressing, I removed the notes from my shirt pocket. Behind the Post-its and the small sketch of the Sillington House there was a fourth piece of paper: a small page from a pocket calendar. The month of October. The fourteenth was circled. Now I knew everything I needed to know except how Julian had slipped that into my pocket.

For the first time since I started school—no, even longer than that—for the first time ever, I was looking forward to a party. And I knew that part of the reason I was looking forward to it was because

Julian had not made it public. Whenever someone makes out a guest list, the people not on it become officially uninvited, and that makes them the enemies of the invited. Guest lists are just a way of choosing sides. The way Julian had done the inviting, I didn't know who else was coming—although I strongly suspected that Nadia Diamondstein would be, and that thought did not displease me.

I wondered if I should bring a gift. It was always better to bring something. I didn't know what. I suspected that sports equipment was out. Books: He probably had as many books as the library. Video game? Wrong. Clothes: NO! Then, when I was in the shower, a word dropped from the showerhead. *Puzzle.* That was it. That was exactly it. A puzzle would be the perfect present for Julian Singh. The video store at the mall had dozens of different puzzles that were not electronic. I had seen three-dimensional puzzles and jigsaw puzzles that had a different picture printed on either side.

I didn't want to tell anyone that I was going to a party. A *tea* party of all things. I hardly believed it myself. I needed a way to get to the mall, so on the Saturday of the party, I asked Mother to please drop me off at the mall on the way home from market. She asked why, as I knew she would, and I told her that I had to buy a present for a party I was going to later that afternoon. Mother was not pleased. She liked to get home right after market so that we could unload the truck and straighten out the accounts. She said all right—not gladly—and told me that she would wait in the truck while I made my purchase.

Why couldn't she come into the mall and browse like a normal woman? Why? Because she knew there was no better way to get me to hurry.

I hopped down from the truck and ran to the video game store. As luck would have it, no salesperson pounced on me the minute I entered. If I had been there to browse, not buy, they would have. Now, I had to practically beg for attention. High on top of the shelves stocked with closed cartons of games of every sort was a display of jigsaw puzzles. There were picture puzzles of waterfalls, 1,000 pieces. There was another one that was a painting of water lilies done in a very loose way. Still another had a picture of a waterfall on one side and a picture of a koala bear on the other. One was a totally white circle. That would be tough because there would be no pattern to help a person line up the pieces. I decided on that one. Two salesclerks were standing at one end of the counter talking. I walked toward them and had to say "Excuse me" twice. I pointed to the puzzle I wanted and said I would like it gift wrapped.

"That's number four-sixty-two. We're all out."

"Then why do you have it on display?"

"It's very popular. We're expecting another shipment next week."

"I need it today," I said. "It's all right with me if you sell me the sample."

"I can't."

"Why? I don't need a discount or anything just because it's the display. I'll pay full price."

The clerk said, "The models are glued together, see, and pasted on a board. So how else do you think they stay up?"

I looked around. "Then I'll take the one that has two different pictures. The one next to the all-white one."

"We're out of that one, too."

"Could you please check your stock in the back?"

"I checked this morning. We don't have it. We have the heart-shaped one in stock."

I looked it over. Instead of a circle, it was shaped like a heart. It was all pink except for a small red heart within the large pink one. Although it wouldn't be quite as difficult as the all-white circle, it, too, would be hard. But it was pink. Pink! Even on Valentine's Day, for a Valentine's Day party, I wouldn't consider giving a pink heart to another guy. "I'll take the water lilies then."

"That's one of our most popular puzzles," the clerk said. "It's a reproduction of a famous painting by an impressionistic French artist who was famous."

"Does that mean you are out of it, too?"

" 'Fraid so."

I thought of Mother waiting in the truck. "Okay," I said, "give me the heart-shaped one. And gift wrap it, please." How could a store that seemed so un-busy be sold out of all the good stuff?

"That will take a while," the clerk said

"Can you hurry? Please?"

"Not if you want me to do a good job."

"Medium," I said. "Can you do a medium job in a hurry?"

The salesclerk smiled and called to her fellow worker. She asked him to do the gift wrap as she rang up the sale. Then while we both waited, she asked, "Is that a present for your girlfriend?"

I knew it. I knew it. My choice was not half wrong; it was all wrong. I was on the verge of asking her to take it back and give me a refund when the clerk emerged from the back room carrying the puzzle box all wrapped in pink paper. I thought I would die. Then I thought of Mother waiting in the truck and asked for a bag to carry it in.

Mother folded the newspaper she was reading. She turned the key in the ignition even before she asked, "What did you get?"

"A puzzle."

"Good idea," she replied.

"Yeah, about twenty minutes ago, I thought so, too."

"By the way, where is this party?"

"The Sillington house."

"Well," Mother said, "I'll bet you'll have good food. I hear that Mr. Singh is a wonderful cook."

"I don't guess I'll be finding that out. I'm only going for tea."

"*For tea?*" Mother asked, a broad smile breaking across her face. "*Tea?*" she repeated.

I wished I could bite off my tongue. How in the world had I let that piece of information escape? "Yes," I said. "For tea. It's a tea party, and tea is always at four."

It would be a good walk—a mile and a half. I could cover three miles in forty-five minutes, so I guessed that I would need a half hour to make it to the Sillington House without a sweat. I was not about to ask Mother to drive me there. I put on a plaid flannel shirt and my best sweater. At the last minute, I put on a necktie. I don't know why I did, and I didn't want to think about it.

Nadia and Julian were on the front porch. They were bending over a small ball of fur. It was a puppy.

"She is Ginger's child," Nadia explained.

"Neat," I replied. I hated saying *Neat*. Nadia's red hair in the autumn light made me forget not to say it.

Mr. Singh came out onto the porch, and Julian made a formal introduction. We shook hands. "How do you like Julian's present from Nadia?" he asked.

I said "awesome" and immediately wished I hadn't.

Mr. Singh held his hand over his brow to make a sunshade and looked into the distance. "That looks like our other guest. Let us welcome him." Then he turned to me and Nadia and asked if we would please excuse him and Julian for a minute.

Nadia and I stood there on the front porch and said nothing to each other. No one would guess that we were almost relatives. We watched Noah Gershom get out of the car and start walking up the brick path to the house. In one hand he held a beautifully wrapped present. I watched Mr. Singh with his white turban and long blue apron over his trousers and Julian at his side walk down the path to greet him. Silhouetted against the sky, they looked like a travel poster for a distant land.

Mr. Singh stepped aside to allow Julian and Noah to precede him up the walk.

Julian took Noah's gift and said, "I believe you know everyone here except Alice."

"Who's Alice?" Noah asked.

Nadia answered. "She is Ginger's daughter. Ginger is my dog, and I have given Julian one of her puppies."

"Did you ask if Julian can have a pet?" Noah asked.

"No," she replied.

"I've never heard someone giving someone a pet for a present without permission."

"I could not believe that anyone would not want one of Ginger's puppies."

"What if Julian has an allergy?"

"If Julian had an allergy—which he does not—he would still want one of Ginger's pups. Ginger is a genius." She looked at me and added, "She is a hybrid genius of unknown I.Q.," and I knew that she was acknowledging our conversation of last summer.

"Oh," Noah said. He hit his forehead with the palm of his hand. "Of course. Of course. I almost forgot. Ginger is the dog that invented $E = mc^2$."

"$E = mc^2$ was not invented. It was discovered, and Einstein discovered it. Ginger is a genius of her genus. She is the best there is of *Canis familiaris*, and Alice is the best of her litter."

"Alice," Noah repeated. "Who named her that?"

"I did," Nadia said. "I thought Julian would like the name because he sent me the invitation to a tea in the book, *Alice's Adventures in Wonderland*."

"I've never heard of someone giving someone a pet for a present without permission and then choosing that pet's name without even asking."

Nadia said, "Well, Noah, now you have. In a single afternoon you have heard of both."

The large center hall of Sillington house had a staircase that curved upward like a stretch of DNA. To the right of the hall was a living room that had a huge fireplace on the end wall; there was no furniture in the room, and the wallpaper was peeling from the walls. On the left of the center hall was the long dining room. I did not remember its having a fireplace, but it did. I was drawn into the room by the large, framed poster over the fireplace mantel.

EXTRAORDINAIRE
SIMONETTA
Chanteuse

Taking up most of the space in the poster was a full-length picture of a smiling, dark-haired woman in a green satin gown. At the bottom was the information:

Appearing Nightly
November 14-29
The Stardust Room

Julian came up behind me. "That is my mother," he said.
"Your mother is a chanteuse?"
"Yes, she was a chanteuse," he said, pronouncing it *shawn-tewz*.
"What does a shawn-tewz do?"
"She sings."
"I saw *The Phantom of the Opera* last summer. There was a wonderful chanteuse in the show."
Julian smiled but said nothing.
"Has she retired?" I asked.
"No," he said. "She died."
"Oh," I said, embarrassed. "I'm sorry."
Julian looked up at the poster. "That poster is quite old. From before my birth. The Stardust Room mentioned there is on a cruise ship. Mother performed there and on other cruise ships. Before it was

necessary for me to start school, I used to travel with Mother and Father. Then I went to boarding school in the north of England in the fall and winter and traveled with them during one of the summer months. Until this year."

"Are you an alien?" I asked.

"Actually, no," he said. "Mother was an American by birth, Father is by naturalization. I was born on the high seas. That makes me American."

"As American as apple pie," I said.

Julian smiled. "Not quite," he said. "Let us say that I am as American as pizza pie. I did not originate here, but I am here to stay." He extended his arm in the direction of Nadia and Noah and took a small step back so that I could pass in front of him. "I think we must join our other guests," he said. "Please," he said. I crossed in front of him, and as I did so, I felt that I was crossing from stage right to stage left and wearing a tuxedo, and I did not mind the feeling at all.

The long trestle tables that are in the picture in the history museum were gone. The dining room was now furnished with two tables-for-two, three tables-for-four, and one larger table at the far end toward the back of the house. Around the tables were an assortment of chairs, none of which matched but seemed to.

The tea was very hot, so we could not gulp it down. We sat at the four sides of a table-for-four and slowly began not to hurry. We sipped the tea and ate small sandwiches that Mr. Singh brought out on a large round tray. Later he brought a three-tiered tray of small pastries. They were delicious, and after finishing hers, Nadia licked her forefinger and with it, picked up the crumbs from her plate. She licked her finger clean so delicately that not even Miss Manners would call it bad.

I, who always preferred silence to speaking, actually started talking. I asked, "How many eighth graders does it take to screw in a light bulb?"

Noah replied, "How many?"

I answered, "Only one. They all know how to screw up."

Everyone laughed.

Noah asked, "Where did you hear that one?"

"I made it up," I confessed. I had made that joke up when light-bulb jokes were popular, but I had never told it to anyone before. I was so pleased with their response to a joke I made up that I told them one I had thought of the day Ham Knapp and Mike Froelich had attacked Julian's book bag.

"What is the difference between a pig sty and the sixth grade?" I asked.

Julian said, "I don't know. What is the difference?"

"In a pig sty an ass is a ham."

Julian quietly said thank you, and no one asked why.

After the tea was gone and the cakes were eaten, Julian opened his presents. Noah's first. A bottle of black, black ink, a pen and a pad of paper marked with double and single lines, and a paperback book.

"For calligraphy," Noah explained. "The ink is called India ink. I thought that would be appropriate."

Julian laughed. "Yes, indeed it is." (Indeed again.) "Calligraphy is a skill I have always wanted to acquire."

"I can teach you," Noah said.

Julian flashed his most dazzling smile at Noah. "I would appreciate that very much," he said.

"Consider it done," Noah replied.

Nadia said, "I have always wanted to write like that. You can teach me, too."

"Do you have the pen?" he asked.

"I will get one." Nadia looked over at me. "Ethan, I think you will feel very left out if you do not get one, too."

"I will make each of you a list of what you need. I'll make the list in calligraphy. Watch me, and it will be your first lesson." Noah filled the pen. It was a very long process. "Filling the pen is not what you do before you begin. It is the beginning," he said. "Learn to make a plus sign so that both the vertical and horizontal strokes are the same thickness. That is your second lesson. You can practice as soon as you buy your materials." We waited and watched as Noah wrote out the two lists.

Before Julian opened up my gift, I knew that it was going to be just right. And it was. "A puzzle!" Julian exclaimed. "I love puzzles. Let's do it now."

So without bothering to clear away our cups and saucers, we took seats at the larger table toward the back of the room. As we began to spread out the pieces of the puzzle, Nadia said, "Just like the Mad Hatter's Tea Party—we all moved one place on."

We worked on the puzzle, each one allowing himself a section of the table and the necessary quiet. Then when all the pieces were used up, we brought our sections together, pushing them left-to-right or right-to-left until they fit together. One piece was missing. We looked on the floor and around the legs of our chairs but didn't find it. I was annoyed with the people who had sold me the puzzle. "They've got their nerve selling defective puzzles," I said.

"But the box was sealed," Noah said.

Julian said, "I think Nadia has it in her hair."

"Do not be ridiculous," Nadia said. "I do not."

"Oh, yes, you do. I see it. Can you see it?" he asked me and Noah. Before we could answer, Julian reached across the table and pulled the last piece of puzzle from Nadia's hair. He held it up between his thumb and forefinger and said, "Dear friends, may I present you with the final solution?" He reached down as if to place the piece of puzzle in the small lake of brown tabletop near the center of the puzzle. But when he opened his hand, out fell three red-and-white-striped mints. "Ah, yes," he said, "I almost forgot our after-tea mints. Please help yourselves." We each picked up a mint, and Julian said, "I think it's time to wrap this up. Ethan," he said, "would you please see if that pesky piece is still in the box?"

I reached down on the floor, opened the box, and there it was—the last piece of puzzle. I took it from the box, put it in place and said, "I'm impressed."

And I was. And so were we all.

The party broke up when Mrs. Gershom arrived to take Noah home. As Noah stood at the front door saying his thank you's, Julian said, "Same time next week. But, please, your presence but not presents."

Noah said, "I've heard that before. As a matter of fact, I've put it in writing."

I left shortly after Noah. The days were getting short, and it was dark when I left the Sillington House. Mrs. Gershom had offered to drive me home, but I wanted to walk. I wanted to walk the road between Sillington House and mine. I wanted to mark the distance slowly. Something had happened at Sillington House. Something made me pull sounds out of my silence the way that Julian pulled puzzle pieces out of Nadia's hair.

Had I gained something at Sillington House? Or had I lost something there? The answer was yes.

The Monday morning following our tea, Julian boarded the bus and said "Good morning" exactly the way he had said it every other day. We did not speak again, and when the bus came to its final stop, we did not wait for each other or walk together into Mrs. Olinski's classroom. That was the way I wanted it. And that was the way it remained.

On Saturday Mother asked me where I was going. I told her. She asked me why, and I said we were working on a project, and that turned out to be the truth.

Mr. Singh was stripping old paper off the walls of one of the bedrooms, and all of us got involved. Mr. Singh had a steamer to loosen the paper from the walls. Noah made a contest out of seeing who could pull off the longest strip. Working quietly on one side of the window, easing the paper off inch by inch, Nadia ended up with a piece that was almost as long as the room was tall. She won.

"What will be my prize?" she asked.

"Ask Noah," I said. "He has a proven talent for thinking of prizes."

"When will I know my prize?" Nadia asked.

"Before our meeting is over," Noah said. "I think I need some tea to think."

When we sat down to our afternoon tea, Nadia proposed that we give ourselves a name.

I thought it was a good idea and suggested, "The Gang of IV. *I*,*V*, the Roman numerals."

Noah said, "No. Nadia gets to choose the name. And that is her prize for pulling off the longest strip of wallpaper. Besides, I think she already has something in mind."

"As a matter of fact, I do," she said. "And swear that as my prize, you will accept my choice."

We said we would.

"Good," she said. "Then it is settled. We are *The Souls*."

"I agree," I said immediately.

Noah cocked his head to one side. "I . . . like . . . it . . . but . . . I think it ought to be the Sillington Souls."

"I did not say that, Noah. I said *The Souls*. Besides, 'Less is more.' "

"What does that mean?" Noah asked. "Less is more. Less is more what? Or less what is more? What does it mean? Less is more."

"Think about it," Nadia said. "If someone hands you a card that says that she is President, Clarion National Bank, it means more than if she hands you a card that says she is First Vice President, Loan Department, Clarion National Bank, Epiphany Branch. If you say *Michelangelo*, it means more than Michelangelo Smith, and just plain *Leonardo* means more than Leonardo Jones."

Noah said, "I don't think you can say *just plain* and apply it to Leonardo."

Nadia said to Noah, "Noah Gershom, you may be smart beyond your years, but you are not wise."

"All right. All right," Noah said. "The Souls." He smiled. "I like it."

"Good," I said, looking over at Julian. "What about you?"

"I agree. We will be The Souls. Let us shake on it."

We rested our elbows on the table's edge and reached toward the center of the table until our hands clutched. "We are now The Souls," Nadia said. When we released our hands, each of us was holding a shiny new penny.

"Ah, yes," Julian said. "If you'll check the date on the coin, you will see they are new—minted in the year The Souls was born."

One Saturday afternoon, shortly after The Souls was born, as we sat around the table-for-four where we had had our tea, I broke the silence by asking—I really don't know why—except that it was something I had been thinking about, "If you could live one day of your life all over again, what day would it be? And why?"

Nadia said, "I would like to live over the morning my father and I helped my grandfather and Margaret rescue the turtles that had been blown ashore by the northeaster." She explained about the turtles, their life cycle, and our walks along the beach up until the morning after the storm. "It was like a scavenger hunt. Ethan was there. Do you remember, Ethan?" I nodded. "For two whole days, we kept them safe in buckets, all covered with wet seaweed. And then Margaret, Grandpa Izzy and my dad, Ethan and I drove to Marineland. Ethan and I kept the buckets between us in the front seat. We were crowded, wet, and messy, and it was fun." She looked over at me, and smiled. "Even your grandmother laughed at the sight of us as we got out of the car." I nodded again. "The marine biologist took us out to the Sargasso Sea, and allowed us to empty the buckets over the edge of the boat. We gave the turtles a lift, and we made it possible for them to continue that phase of their life. It was a most wonderful day. Remember, Ethan?"

I remembered.

Noah said, "I would like to live over the day I was best man at a wedding in Century Village that involved four grandparents—two of mine and one each of two other Souls."

Noah had a knack for telling a story, and all of us laughed, even the two of us who already knew the details. Nadia, who had not found the details funny before, found them funny now.

Julian, ever polite, asked, "Is it now my turn?"

Nadia said, "Please."

Julian picked up a deck of cards. He spoke as he shuffled. "If I could repeat one day of my life," he said, pushing the cards across the table to Noah. "Cut them, please." Noah did, and Julian nodded. "I would choose the time we were sailing back to England," he said as he began to deal the cards, going round and round. "All during the journey from the Mediterranean, Gopal, who did close-up magic, had been teaching me how to play poker." Julian looked over the table and counted the cards—three—at each place. Then he slowly dealt another round as he continued talking. "Finally on the day we docked at Southampton, the very day before I was to start boarding school . . ." Julian smiled, laid the remaining deck of cards in the middle of the table, and said, "Would you mind turning over your cards?"

We did. I, who was on Julian's left had four two's; Noah, who was next had four three's; Nadia had four four's. Julian said, "On the day we docked at Southampton, Gopal said something to me . . ." Julian turned over two of the top cards from the remaining deck: Aces. "On the day we docked, Gopal said that I had chops." Julian turned over the next two cards: Two more aces. "That day when Gopal told me that I had chops, that is the day I would like to live over."

We applauded.

"What are chops?" Nadia asked

"Chops," Julian said, "is to magic what doing scales is to a chanteuse. Without it you cannot be a magician, with it alone you cannot be an artist."

Something in Sillington House gave me permission to do things I had never done before. Never even thought of doing. Something there triggered the unfolding of those parts that had been incubating. Things that had lain inside me, curled up like the turtle hatchlings newly emerged from their eggs, taking time in the dark of their nest to unfurl themselves. I told jokes I had never told before. I asked questions I had never asked before. When it was my turn to tell what day I would like to live over, after Nadia had finished, after Noah and Julian had, too, I told mine.

The Souls listened and were not embarrassed to hear, and I was not embarrassed to say, "I would like to live over the day of our first tea party. And, look," I added, "every Saturday since, I get to do just that."

Four

M RS. OLINSKI SAT, waiting, until all the members of her class were seated. Then she introduced herself. "I am Mrs. Olinski. I am one of those people who gets to use all those good parking spaces at the mall." She turned toward the blackboard and wrote in big, block letters:

MRS. OLINSKI
PARAPLEGIC

As she wrote *paraplegic*, Mrs. Olinski spelled it out, "P-A-R-A-P-L-E-G-I-C. It means that I am paralyzed from the waist down."

Mrs. Olinski had thought about what she would say to this, her first sixth-grade class in ten years. She wrote it all down, revised, memorized, and rehearsed until she could deliver her lines with a light touch. Her voice held steady, but her hands did not, and the O of Olinski was the rough shape of an oil spill.

Then a student in the back—Hamilton Knapp—stood up. "Excuse me, Mrs. Olinski," he said, hesitating slightly, mispronouncing her name. "I can't see what you've written. Could you write a little higher on the blackboard, please?"

Mrs. Olinski replied, "Not at the moment," and managed an embarrassed smile. The rest of her prepared remarks flew out of her head. She thought she had thought of everything. But here she was with a problem about sight lines to the blackboard. Given time, she would figure it out, but she wished it had not come up on the very first hour of her very first day back.

After Hamilton Knapp sat down, she laughed nervously. "I was about to tell you that being a paraplegic does not mean that there is anything wrong with my hearing or my eyesight, but I guess we'll have to figure out what to do about the eyesight of those of you who will be seated in the back of the room."

Mrs. Olinski decided that she would write nothing more on the blackboard for the rest of the morning but would leave what she had already written right there so that she could check it out after lunch. She would return before the rest of the class, wheel herself to the back of the room while it was still empty, and check out the sight lines.

She took the roll, checking on the spelling and pronunciation of each child's name, and passed out general supplies and the books for the social studies she would be teaching. Finally, she assigned seats in alphabetical order, last names first.

The year of her accident, Mrs. Olinski had had two Jennifers in her class. This semester, Jennifer was out of fashion, and J-names for boys were in. She had J-names from Jared to Julian, including two Jasons. When she returned from lunch and saw CRIPPLE written on the blackboard, she knew more than the names had changed. Sixth graders had changed.

* * *

Ethan finished answering the four-part question about the history of the state of New York. ". . . the first women's rights convention organized by Elizabeth Cady Stanton. Auburn was the home of Harriet Tubman who ran the underground railroad."

"That registers six points for the Epiphany Team," the commissioner said. There was a spontaneous burst of applause from their side of the aisle that was immediately suppressed by the commissioner. "I must admonish the audience not to applaud. It is distracting to both teams."

Mrs. Olinski remembered the day that rude applause had distracted a performance. Her fourth choice had been causing her problems, but it had been on the very day when rude applause interrupted a play that she had made the fourth and final choice for her team.

* * *

It was the Saturday afternoon after they became The Souls, sometime after they had finished their four o'clock tea, when Julian had said, "We must have a project," and Noah had asked, "Isn't peeling wallpaper enough?"

Julian grinned and said no. He took a small object from his pants pocket and kept it hidden in his fist. He rested his hands lightly on the edge of the table.

"And the calligraphy lessons. Aren't they enough?" Julian said no again, and Noah asked, "Now what?"

Nadia said, "I think Julian already has something in mind."

"Indeed I do." Julian turned his fist over and opened his hand. There within his palm was a small ivory monkey, only two inches high. He laid it on the table and waited until each of The Souls had inspected it thoroughly before saying, "Gopal gave me this little sculpture. It can do tricks." Julian then stood the little figure first on one foot, then the other; one arm, then the other. "You see, this monkey can balance on any one of its four limbs."

Noah asked, "What is that supposed to mean?"

Ethan replied, "I think it has something to do with Mrs. Olinski."

Julian smiled broadly. "Indeed it does."

"Mrs. Olinski?" Noah repeated. "Mrs. Olinski? What?"

"I think that Julian wants us to help her," Ethan explained.

"Help her do what?" Noah asked.

Nadia said, "Stand on her own two feet. Have you never heard that expression, Noah?"

"Of course, I have heard that expression, but fact: Mrs. Olinski cannot stand on her own two feet and further fact: she obviously . . ." Noah's voice trailed off as he understood. "I get it," he said. "I get it. It is scary trying to stand on your own two feet especially when you don't have a leg to stand on, so to speak."

Julian rubbed the little ivory monkey. "There are some in the school who try to get her off balance. Some are in our homeroom."

"We can give her some support," Ethan said.

"Better than that," Nadia said, "we can give her a lift."

They all turned to Noah. "What do you suggest?" they asked, knowing Noah would have an answer. And he did.

* * *

The commissioner reached into the bowl again. He allowed his hand to touch bottom before spreading his fingers to pick up the next question. "An acronym is defined as a word formed from the initial letters of a series of words. For example, RADAR is an acronym for RAdio Detecting And Ranging. R-A from *radio*, D from *detecting*, A from *and*, and R from *ranging*. Can you give me two more examples of acronyms that have entered our language as words?"

Julian Singh's buzzer went off. "Posh and tip," he called out.

Julian Narrates When Ginger Played Annie's Sandy

It was the Saturday of Thanksgiving weekend that Ethan Potter suggested to Nadia Diamondstein that she have Ginger play Annie's Sandy. I had no idea what he was talking about. I knew, of course, that Ginger referred to Nadia's beloved and talented dog, so I thought that perhaps *Annie's Sandy* was a video game played by the canine orders. However, the word *play* referred to playing a part in a musical show about an orphan named Annie in a show called *Annie*, and Sandy was the name of the dog belonging to the title character. Epiphany High School was putting on the play for The Holiday Season. Until we moved to Epiphany, I had no idea how busy Americans are between Thanksgiving and New Year's Day, the time they refer to as The Holiday Season. Everyone asks, "Are you ready for the holidays?" And then afterward, they ask, "How were your holidays?" During the holidays themselves, no one asks about them.

When Ethan suggested that Nadia have Ginger try out, Nadia said, "Ginger does not do Arf." Another remark I did not understand. I did not intend to ask. I knew that if I waited, an explanation would come. It did.

The play, *Annie*, is based on an American comic strip called "Little Orphan Annie," and when Annie's Sandy speaks, in the balloon over his head is written *Arf!* Everyone had already been cast for the high school production but not the dog Sandy, and Mrs. Reynolds, the play's director, had put a notice on the bulletin board that anyone with a well-trained dog could try out.

Ethan said, "They call that a 'cattle call.' "

Noah said, "Why would they call it a cattle call, if they are asking for dogs?"

Ethan said, "It's a theatrical saying. It means an open audition. Even if they mean people, they call it a cattle call."

"Then what do they call a cattle call?" Noah asked.

Ethan replied, "A round-up, I guess." He turned to Nadia and said, "Ginger's bark will do very well. Besides, she looks a lot like Sandy except that her eyeballs aren't blank." (In time I came to understand that remark, too. The artist who drew the comic strip never drew irises on the eyes of people or dogs.)

Noah said, "There is one other thing."

Nadia ignored Noah. She said to Ethan, "If I do have Ginger try out, she will get the part. Ginger is a genius."

Noah said, "There is one other thing."

Nadia turned to Noah and said, "Ginger is a genius. She will get the part."

"Nadia, my dear," Noah insisted, "Sandy is a male, and fact: Ginger is a—if you'll excuse the expression—a bitch. From everything I've ever learned in health education, genes, not genius, determine—if you'll excuse the expression—sex. Fact: Unless Ginger visits a plastic surgeon, she won't fit the part."

Nadia said, "Noah, is there any subject in this whole world that you do not know more about than every other being on this planet?"

Noah shrugged. "Not every other being on the planet. Let's just say, 'Every other being in this room.' "

"Do you have a dog?" she asked.

"No, but . . ."

"Just answer the question. Do you have a dog?"

"No, but . . ."

"Just answer the question. Have you ever had a dog?"

"No, but . . ."

"Just answer the question. Have you ever had a dog?"

"No."

Nadia said, "I rest my case."

Noah would not give up. "Have you ever had allergies that kept you from having a dog?" he asked.

"No."

"Have you ever had a brother who had allergies that kept you from having a dog?"

"No, I have not and neither have you."

"Have you ever had a brother?"

"No."

"I . . ."

Ethan interrupted. "Getting back to Ginger. You ought to let her try out."

Nadia said, "I shall. She will get the part, and they will consider themselves lucky, which they should, because Ginger is a genius."

The bickering between Nadia and Noah no longer made me

uncomfortable. As a matter of fact, I had begun to enjoy it. And so had we all, including Noah and Nadia.

Once Nadia made her decision to have Ginger try out for the part, I told them that in the days when I had traveled with my parents on the cruise line, I saw a number of animal acts. There were not many, for keeping animals on board ship is not easy. I explained that wild animals were out of the question as were the larger varieties of domestic animal such as cow or horse. There was a monkey, once, but it was a terrible thief. The monkey whose name was Sapphire (his hind quarters were bright blue) would swing down from a flagpole or a railing and steal shiny objects like pens or barrettes or, even worse, jewelry. Sapphire always would drink anything that was left unattended in a cup or a glass. As a result Sapphire was often drunk and incapable of bladder control. Most passengers were not amused, and the captain had Sapphire and his owner put off the ship at the next port.

"Most of the animal acts on board ship involved dogs," I explained. "From watching them I learned what trainers do."

So it was that even before the cattle call, The Souls began the intensive training of Ginger.

I taught each of The Souls how to palm a treat so that no one in the audience would notice. First, we taught Ginger to respond to Nadia, and then Nadia fused with Ethan and then Ethan with Noah, then Noah with me until at last Ginger would respond to the treat and not the person. We trained Ginger to accept the treat without excessive salivating. Most people who are not dog owners, and even many who are, do not care very much for a tongue bath.

Ethan got a copy of the script. In the play, the policeman asks, "Is that your dog, little girl?" and Sandy is supposed to bark. We taught Ginger to bark on cue, and the more she did it, the more it sounded like Arf!

Ginger had learned her lines. Ginger had learned her cues. Ginger was a genius.

Eight dogs, their owners, the entire cast of the play, and The Souls attended the dog try-outs. I had thought about bringing Alice, but Papa advised against it. He said that a daughter should not be in competition with her mother, but I think he would have missed her during the times she would be at rehearsals. Alice and Papa kept each other company when I was at school. Alice had become our early-warning system. Every time someone started up the path to Sillington House, Alice barked to let us know. We were a little concerned that when we had paying guests, which would be soon, this might be a problem.

One of the eight dogs was quickly eliminated on grounds of disobedience. The second had a problem with his plumbing, and Mrs. Reynolds was not amused by the snickers in the audience or the mess on stage. The next two were small, nervous creatures that looked like battery-operated plush toys. They did not run in a straight line but zigzagged and yipped their way across the stage. Numbers five and six were male and did embarrassing things to legs, any legs—male or female—that happened to be onstage. The two remaining contenders were Ginger and Michael Froelich's dog, Arnold. Arnold, a well-behaved yellow Labrador retriever, was larger than Ginger and was—quite decidedly and obviously—male.

I wanted Ginger to get the part, not only because she belonged to Nadia and not only because she was Alice's mother but also because I did not want Michael Froelich to have the honor. Since those first weeks at school, I had done my best to avoid both Michael Froelich and his friend, Hamilton Knapp.

Arnold tried out before Ginger. The girl who was to play Annie stood center stage, clapped her hands upon her thighs, and Arnold leaped across the stage, placed his paws upon Annie's shoulders, and caused her to lean backward. She almost fell. Froelich ran across the stage and quickly hooked a leash to Arnold's collar and said to Stage-Annie, "I promise you that won't happen again, but it will help if you dig your heels in a little."

Mrs. Reynolds, the drama teacher, said, "Next."

It was Ginger's turn, and Stage-Annie once again clapped her hands on her knees. Nadia quietly whispered, "Go, Ginger," gave her a little push on her rump and quickly crossed to the other side of the stage behind the backdrop and stood in the wings on the opposite side of the stage where no one in the audience could see her, but Ginger could. In between stood Stage-Annie, holding a treat.

Privately, before try-outs began, I had slipped backstage and taught Stage-Annie how to palm a treat and pass it off so that no one in the audience could see. Ginger walked across the stage with enthusiasm and dignity and quietly nuzzled Stage-Annie's hand before sitting at her feet.

Ginger was in every way clearly superior to every other dog there.

Even her mixed-breed looks better suited the part than Arnold's pure-bred sleekness. Ginger was first rate. Ginger had star quality. Ginger got the part.

Mrs. Reynolds, the drama coach who was director of the play, said, "Ginger will be Annie's Sandy, and Arnold will be Ginger's understudy."

We Souls, sitting in the audience, applauded, and Ethan stood and yelled, "Bravo! Mrs. Reynolds. Bravo!" Ethan had always wanted to stand up in a theater and yell *Bravo!*

Mrs. Reynolds said, "Who is doing that yelling?"

Ethan waved his hand and called out, "It's me, Mrs. Reynolds. Me. Here. Ethan Potter."

Mrs. Reynolds shielded her eyes from the footlights to see out over the audience. "Ethan Potter?" Still screening her eyes, she smiled. "Ethan Potter. I didn't recognize you." I believe that she did not recognize him for the person yelling *Bravo!* was Ethan, The Soul—not Ethan, the silent. Then she asked, "How is your grandmother, Ethan?"

"She's fine, Mrs. Reynolds. She got married last summer."

"I heard," Mrs. Reynolds replied. "And how is that big brother of yours? How's Lucas?"

"He's fine, Mrs. Reynolds."

"Will you tell him I said hello?"

"Yes, I will."

"When will you see him again?"

"He'll be home for Christmas."

"I hope he'll come see the play," she said. "Will you tell him?"

"Yes, I will."

Ethan did not say another word until we left the auditorium that day.

Ginger learned to bark Arf! on cue and quickly won the hearts of the entire cast as well as Mrs. Reynolds. Nadia was beaming.

Nadia had kindly passed along training information to Froelich and to Stage-Annie, and Arnold's performance improved to within a shade of Ginger's. It would have been better if Arnold had been eliminated altogether. Second best can be worse than not-in-the-running. Who knew what was happening inside Froelich's head as he trained Arnold. Who knew what was happening inside Froelich's head when he attended rehearsals—he had to attend them all—and had nothing to do except to wait backstage and watch admiration and affection be heaped on Ginger. That amounted to a lot of work for little glory. During the actual performances he and Arnold were to stay backstage and out of sight—unless something happened to Ginger. Did having Arnold as understudy make Froelich feel like an underdog?

I was not without worry.

The main performance was to be on Saturday evening before the winter recess. That was when friends and family would attend. This event was exciting for Papa and me not only because Alice's mother was about to make her dramatic debut but also because Sillington House was, too. Mr. and Mrs. Diamondstein where flying up from Florida to celebrate Christmas with the Potters and would be our first paying guests. They planned to arrive in time to see Ginger play Annie's Sandy.

Papa had only one of the guest bedrooms ready, but he was quite proud of it, and so was I. He hung the bed linen out on a clothesline he strung across the backyard so that everything would smell of the sweet air that blew off the lake. He purchased a beautiful cut glass carafe and matching drinking glass and put them on the nightstand by the bed. He purchased a poinsettia and put it on the dresser. In the closet were the heavy hangers of polished wood—not those permanently attached things that you find in cheap motels nor the weak wire ones you get from the dry cleaners—that Papa had bought in England. We had them all facing the same way so that their shadows on the wall looked like a computer rendering of an architectural cross section. The sink and tub were scrubbed until their whiteness could snow-blind. The faucets shone bright enough to use as mirrors.

The Diamondsteins arrived on Friday afternoon before the official start of the school holiday. That was the afternoon that I and all other members of the elementary and middle schools of Epiphany were to attend a special matinee performance of *Annie*. For the cast it would be something more than a full dress rehearsal because of a full live audience.

Everyone at Epiphany Middle School was to be transported to the high school by bus. That meant walkers and car-poolers were all going by bus so that our usual seating arrangement was not in order. I had a window seat.

Jared Lord had the window seat two rows in front of me. Ham Knapp took the seat next to him. Ever since the first few weeks of school, when I could not avoid Knapp and his friends, I did my best to ignore them. But I was never unaware of them. Since I had become a Soul and since Froelich had started attending rehearsals, I had become less concerned about him, but Ham was another matter. I was never, never unaware of him or any of his friends. Whenever Knapp was anywhere nearby, all my senses were on alert.

Even though it was late December, the sun, pouring in through the windows of the bus as it waited in the car park, had heated it up like a greenhouse. We were dressed in woolens, so we opened the windows before sitting down for the ride to the high school. I mention all of this because as soon as the bus started out of the car park, the wind coming through the open windows of the bus caused a peculiar warp in the sound.

The first word I heard was *tranquilizer*. It flowed out of one window and back in through mine as clearly as if Ham Knapp were sitting in the seat next to me.

I rested my head against the window post and began to listen intently. The woof of wind produced by cars approaching in the opposite direction caused some blanks in the conversation, but I heard enough.

. . . tranquilizer and laxative . . .

How did you . . .

. . . sent biscuits . . . doggie treats . . . for the star dog.

. . . laxative and tranquilizers and those four little legs will buckle, and those little bowels won't hold . . . There followed some laughter and some mumbling.

Nadia had told The Souls about Ginger's bad reaction to tranquilizers during her trip to Florida last August. She could very well have told this to everyone including Froelich. Froelich could have told Knapp, or Knapp could have heard it himself, for Nadia enjoyed talking about Ginger.

Tranquilizers and laxatives . . . Pass out like a mop. Instant coma. What's the point? She'll pass out backstage.

. . . point is that star dog Ginger is out and buddy dog Arnold is in.

It was clear Ham meant harm to Ginger.

No problem . . . Mother keeps a supply . . .

Why would his mother keep a supply of animal tranquilizers at home?

. . . easy . . . gave them to Nadia . . . gift from my mother. . .

Of course! Knapp's mother was a veterinarian, the owner and operator of Vet in a Van. On several occasions I had seen the van bring Ham to school. The van was painted with the Vet in a Van logo and beneath it was written: Pat Knapp, DVM. I had assumed that Dr. Pat Knapp was a man and that his mother had borrowed the car. It had not occurred to me that his mother was the vet in the van.

It took no great leap of intelligence to realize that Hamilton Knapp had laced Ginger's dog treats with tranquilizers and laxatives so that she would do one, possibly two, embarrassing things on stage. He gave Nadia the drugged treats and told her that they were a gift from Dr. Knapp, who was Ginger's veterinarian. I could easily picture Hamilton Knapp telling Nadia that Dr. Knapp wanted Ginger to have these special treats for her performance. Nadia was so crazy about Ginger that she would believe that anyone who met her wanted to give her gifts.

As soon as the bus stopped, I made my way forward and slipped a Year-of-the-Souls penny into Noah's hand. In the crush at the bus door, I had time to whisper, "Backstage emergency. Cover for me." For reasons we had not spoken of, yet each of us understood, none of us was ready to reveal our association. I watched Noah make his way toward Ethan and pass a Soul penny to him. He had understood. I knew he would.

Just inside the auditorium, Noah bent down to tie his shoe, and Ethan tripped over him. They caused enough confusion for me to slip back outside and run around toward the back of the building and enter the auditorium through the stage door.

I was backstage.

I stayed in the shadow of the wings for a minute until I could get my bearings. The cast was jabbering, tugging at their clothes, too excited about themselves to pay attention to anyone else.

The first time Ginger appears onstage, she is running in front of the dog catcher. She is supposed to be a stray, and her fur must look matted and dirty. Nadia accomplished this by wetting portions of

Ginger's fur and tamping them down. For the audience, the wet spots look dark and dirty. For Ginger's second appearance, she wears a rope leash, and for her final appearance, a scene in which Ginger and Annie have taken up residence at the mansion of the wealthy Daddy Warbucks, Ginger-as-Sandy appears clean and brushed and wears a rhinestone collar and red ribbon around her neck. Between acts Nadia has time to dry Ginger's fur and brush her until her coat glistens.

Backstage between the wings stood the prop table where Nadia kept the big red bow and rhinestone collar, the hair dryer, the rope and the treats that Stage-Annie uses to entice Ginger. I saw the table and worked my way invisibly through the backstage crowd, a technique I had learned from Gopal when I helped him with his act on board the cruise ship.

The treats were already laid out on the props table. I saw the rope. I also saw a fancy collar, but it was wider than Ginger's and the red bow was different. I examined the treats. They, too, were different. They were shaped like strips of bacon. Ginger's usual treats were shaped like small bones. I was sure that these were drugged. I edged my way over to the table to pick up the dog biscuits and throw them away. I would destroy these treats, and then, if time and opportunity allowed, I would find Nadia's supply and substitute good ones for the drugged ones.

If time and opportunity did not allow, then Ginger would have to go into her act without a bribe. I would count on Ginger's genius.

Before I had a change to scoop up the bacon-shaped treats from the table, I saw Froelich and Arnold coming out of the boys' dressing room. Arnold was wet down and not wearing his collar or dog tags. Mrs. Reynolds was waiting outside the boys' dressing room. She smiled and said something to Froelich and then called, "Places, everyone."

As the backstage crowd started breaking up, I saw Nadia: She was holding Ginger's leash and carrying the shopping bag where she kept her props. Ginger was still wearing her regular collar and dog tags.

Had something already happened to Ginger?

It was only minutes to curtain. I changed directions and slipped back into the shadow of the wings. I waited until Nadia came within a few feet of where I stood. I came forward, slipped a Year-of-the-Souls penny into her hand, and immediately returned to the shadows.

Nadia gave no indication that she had the penny, but she was at my side in less then a minute.

"Is Ginger all right?" I asked.

"She is fine," she said, shortening her leash and laying the shopping bag down on the floor. She reached down to pet Ginger. "Ginger is having a day off. It was Mrs. Reynolds's idea. Mike Froelich has been so good about coming to rehearsals, and Arnold has become so well trained that Mrs. Reynolds decided to let him play Sandy at this performance."

"Oh," I said, "when did you find out?"

"Just this morning. Do not worry. Arnold is only a substitute. Ginger will appear at all of the evening performances."

"So the treats on the props table are Arnold's not Ginger's?"

"In a manner of speaking. Our vet sent them over for Ginger, but since Arnold is performing today, I gave him some. We both use the same vet."

The treats awaiting Arnold were drugged. Neither Michael nor Nadia knew it. And Hamilton Knapp did not know that Arnold, not Ginger, was about to consume them.

I could save Arnold from the poisoned treats, let him go on, and let Knapp think that his dirty trick had worked. One for the price of two. Or I could let Arnold eat the drugged treats, embarrass Froelich, and let Ginger go on. Two for the price of one.

There they were, waiting on the prop table. There they were, waiting for my decision.

"Why are you here, Julian?" Nadia asked.

"To wish you 'Break a leg,' " I said. " 'Break a leg' is what you say to theater people instead of good luck."

"And what do you say to theater dogs?" she asked.

"You double it. You say, 'Break two legs.' "

Nadia laid her shopping bag down at my feet and tugged at Ginger's leash. "Come along, Ginger," she said, "let us go wish some people to break some legs."

I watched them walk away.

I made my decision.

I waited in the dark of the wing until the orchestra was well into playing the overture, for then I knew that the houselights would be lowered, and I could make my way to my seat unnoticed. Noah and

Ethan had propped their jackets and backpacks on an aisle seat so that the shadow cast in the darkened auditorium could easily be mistaken for a person. I slipped into the seat, nodded to both Noah and Ethan, and waited for Sandy's first appearance on stage.

The first time Sandy appeared, running across the stage being chased by the dog catcher, the audience broke into spontaneous applause. They were already in love. The second time, the policeman asked, "Is that your dog, little girl?" and Sandy walked across the stage and sat at Stage-Annie's feet, and once again the audience broke into applause. This time, however, when the applause was about to die down, Knapp and Lord exchanged a triumphant look and began barking, "Arf! Arf! Arf!" and clapping in rhythm. Soon all the other kids picked up on that, and the play could not continue.

Senior monitors started fanning down the aisles to locate the source of the trouble, but before the monitor was even with their row, Knapp's hands were folded in his lap; his lips, sealed.

When the play was finished and after all the players had taken a bow, Arnold-as-Sandy walked in front of all the actors and sat down, center stage. The red bow had slipped from the back of his neck to the side. He sat downstage, center, for only a second before glancing over his shoulder, getting up, and walking a few steps upstage to line up with the other players. Stage-Annie and Daddy Warbucks took a step to the right and to the left respectively to make room for him. Arnold looked out over the audience, sitting in a circle of light, and the audience went wild.

They stood, began clapping in rhythm to their chant, *SAN-dy, SAN-dy, SAN-dy.* Knapp and Lord picked up the beat and started an undertone of *Arf! Arf! Arf!* and soon the audience became a two-part chorus with half the auditorium chanting SAN-dy, and the other half responding with ARF, ARF in a manner more suited to an athletic contest than musical theater. The curtain was dropped, the house lights came on, and the chanting softened, faded, and died. Knapp and Lord exchanged a satisfied look.

Mrs. Reynolds walked onstage and stood in front of the curtain. She held a microphone in her hand and hissed into it, "Sit-t-t-t down!"

THUMP-THUMP-THUMP-THUMP-THUMP-MP-MP-MP— the sound of hundreds of bottoms hitting hundreds of seats followed.

Mrs. Reynolds waited until an embarrassed silence fell over the auditorium. "Part of the theater experience is learning to be a good audience. You have not been a good audience. You have been a very bad one. I am sorry that you have not learned at home how to act in public. I am ashamed for you because I know you are not ashamed for yourselves. I would like you to leave. Now. You can start correcting your behavior by leaving this auditorium in a quiet and orderly fashion."

Suddenly senior monitors appeared at the end of every third row, and we quietly and slowly made our way toward the exit. The auditorium was almost empty by the time we reached the exit. Mrs. Olinski was sitting in her chair between doors. She called my name. "Julian. Julian Singh," she called, "I would like to see you a minute."

Had she seen me slip backstage? Or did she think that I started that ruckus in the auditorium? My school days are over, I thought. I will be expelled, I thought. How will I break the news to Papa?

Mrs. Olinski said, "I understand you have guests at Sillington House."

"Yes, ma'am, we do. Mr. and Mrs. Diamondstein were due to arrive from Florida this afternoon."

"Mrs. Diamondstein is an old friend of mine. She asked me to stop by and meet her new husband. How would you like to ride home with me?" she asked.

I was so relieved that I could not speak. I answered by nodding my head like one of those nodding animals that Americans put on the rear ledge of their automobiles.

Ethan, who was just behind me, said, "May I come, too? Mrs. Diamondstein is my grandma Draper."

"Yes, so she is. I had almost forgotten. Of course, you may come."

"Let me go backstage and get Nadia," Ethan suggested. "Mr. Diamondstein is her grandfather."

Mrs. Olinski laughed. "It seems all of our sixth grade is one happy family. Go ahead," she said. "Go backstage and tell Nadia to meet us at my van."

A voice that was midway out the door called, "Can I come, too?"

"You, Noah? What reason do you have?" Mrs. Olinski asked.

"Me?" Noah asked. "You want to know what reason I have for coming along?"

Mrs. Olinski smiled patiently.

"Well, Mrs. Olinski, my reason is the best of all. Fact: I was best man at their wedding."

Mrs. Olinski laughed. "Were you really?"

"Yes, I was. I'll tell you about it. I'll spare no detail."

Mrs. Olinski laughed. "Then, by all means, Noah, you must come along."

Noah grinned. "I have always wanted to ride in a handicapped van. All my life, I have wanted to see how a disabled person like your-self applies the brakes and steps on the gas."

Mrs. Olinski said, "I don't exactly *step* on the gas."

"There you go!" Noah said. "This is precisely what I would like to see. I would precisely like to see exactly how you *apply* the gas."

Mrs. Olinski said, "That is either the most honest or the most dis-honest answer I have ever heard. I must notify the bus driver that I'll be driving you four souls home."

Why did she say that? She was smiling. Did she know that we were The Souls? Did she know? Noah caught my eye and quickly changed the subject. "You'll have to take Ginger home, too, Mrs. Olinski. If you don't mind, of course. You don't have to have any special fittings in the van to transport animals. It's a good thing, too. Now, if Ginger were a seeing-eye dog . . ."

Mrs. Olinski interrupted. "Noah," she said, "run down to the bus and tell Mrs. Korshak that I will be along in a minute. I have a mes-sage for her."

"I'd be happy to give her that message, Mrs. Olinski."

"I'm sure you would, but the message involves permissions that I, not you, have the authority to give." Noah started down the row of yellow buses, and Mrs. Olinski followed.

There had been a moment backstage when I had been tempted to allow Arnold to eat the drugged treats. That had been the same mo-ment that I thought it would be satisfying to get even with Froelich and Knapp. But then I was able mentally to separate Froelich from Knapp and Arnold from both of them, so I slipped over to the props table, scooped up all the poisoned treats, and put them in my right pocket. At the same time I substituted Ginger's wholesome treats— treats I had taken from Nadia's shopping bag—from my left pocket.

The drugged treats were still in my pocket.

Ethan, Nadia, and Ginger had not yet come out of the auditorium. Noah and Mrs. Olinski had gone to speak to Mrs. Korshak. I stood alone. There was something I wanted to do. When Knapp had started that ruckus, I had momentarily regretted my decision to save Arnold. I was still so angry that I was about to violate one of the cardinal rules that Gopal had taught me.

I walked out onto the street so that no one on the sidewalk would notice as I made my way down the line of buses waiting—headlight to taillight—by the curb. Beyond them was the line of cars waiting for pickups. Traffic could go only one way, and no one was allowed to make a U-turn, so even those cars that had already picked up their riders were stuck, waiting for buses to load.

Gopal had taught me that magicians never reveal the secrets of their trade to laymen. Gopal always said that magicians who were interested in letting people know how clever they were were not really magicians. "Don't ever destroy the wonder," Gopal had said. "Let your magic show you off, not you show off your magic."

I knew that Hamilton Knapp would find out soon enough that Arnold, not Ginger, had been chosen for the afternoon's performance. He would find out soon enough that his trick had not worked. I knew that I should never reveal to Hamilton Knapp that I had saved Arnold from the fate he had meant for Ginger. I knew all of that. Yet I moved toward the Vet in a Van. Dr. Knapp was behind the wheel, waiting for her turn to pull out. I walked around the back of the van onto the sidewalk on the passenger's side. I tapped on the window and motioned for Ham to roll it down. I reached into the open window. He pulled away from me but said nothing.

"What's the matter?" his mother said.

"Your son has something growing out of his head," I said as I pulled two bacon-shaped doggie treats from his ears. "I think these belong to you," I said as one by one I dropped the rest of the drugged biscuits on his lap. I turned and walked away.

I was glad that I had chops. Gopal would forgive me.

Five

THE DEADLINE for choosing an academic team was the Tuesday following the winter holiday. The other homeroom teachers were ready by Thanksgiving. They had held mini contests in their classrooms and had selected the winners of those. They had ready answers for anyone who asked how they had chosen their teams. In the teachers' lounge, Mrs. Sharkey, who taught sixth grade math, accused Mrs. Olinski of being dictatorial, and Ms. Masolino, who taught music and who did not have a homeroom at all, hinted that she was lazy. Mrs. Olinski did not take kindly to these remarks. Her voice quavering, she answered her critics. "I have my reasons," she said, even though she knew she didn't. Something stronger than reason was having its way with her, and she didn't know what that was either.

Mrs. Laurencin, Epiphany Middle School principal, called Mrs. Olinski into the office one afternoon and quietly warned her that she better have a good answer for the parents of any high honor roll student who didn't make her team. Mrs. Olinski said, "By the time they get to sixth grade, honor roll students won't risk making a mistake, and sometimes to be successful, you have to risk making mistakes." Mrs. Laurencin agreed with her but warned her that that would not be a very popular reason. "Furthermore," Mrs. Olinski added, "sometimes we even have to risk making fools of ourselves." Mrs. Laurencin never approved of that answer either.

Even though Mrs. Olinski could not tell why, she could tell when she decided not to hold try-outs. It was on a Saturday in late October, some time after four o'clock. She had been correcting social studies papers and had just finished reading Noah Gershom's essay on the First Amendment when the thought flew into her head. She would appoint her team, the way the president appointed his cabinet. She made her decision. Just. Like. That.

She chose Noah right away, and almost immediately after, she thought of Nadia and Ethan. They looked like strong candidates. She would watch them and see.

In the weeks that followed, she became more convinced of their being right for the job. She had not yet officially notified any of them because she wanted to make all four appointments at the same time, and the fourth was causing problems.

She had been considering asking Hamilton Knapp—yes, *that* Hamilton Knapp. Although he was naughty, he was also smart, and bad boys had always held a certain charm for her. But each time something told her he was the right choice, something else told her he was wrong. So she held back.

While she waffled between asking Ham and not asking him, she never gave a thought to asking Julian Singh. He was smart (or else his English accent made him seem so). And he was sophisticated (or else his English accent made him seem so). But Julian Singh was too far off the mainland. He was an island unto himself, definitely not a team player. Ham Knapp was a leader. Ham Knapp had friends. But Julian stood alone. Just as he had stood alone the fist day of school at the blackboard in front of the word CRIPPLE.

On the day the Epiphany Middle School was invited to attend *Annie*, Mrs. Olinski had driven her van to the high school and had arrived ahead of the school bus. She waited at the foot of the steps as the kids filed out. She saw Julian Singh push his way forward and then scurry down the steps and out of sight. He had disappeared into thin air. She didn't want to call into thin air and look to all the world (and all the other teachers) as if she had no control of her class. Mrs. Olinski was annoyed with Julian Singh. Once inside the auditorium, she had looked for him again but had been unable to spot him before the house lights dimmed, and the show got under way.

Then Sandy appeared on stage, and the clapping and the chanting *Arf! Arf! Arf!* had started in the section of the auditorium where her class was seated. From where she had been sitting, in a handicapped space by the exit, she could not see who had started it, but she knew one of her students was responsible. She knew it, and she was angry. Mrs. Olinski had a great tolerance for mischief, but she had no patience for malice. This was not mischief. There is a playful quality to mischief. This was malice. There is a mean quality to malice. Someone in her class was terribly mean.

When the lights went on, and Mrs. Reynolds stormed on stage to scold the audience, Mrs. Olinski was able to wheel herself around to examine her students. With a sick feeling in her stomach, she scanned them one at a time. Like the cursor on a computer screen her eyes moved from the first row to the second, then stopped. Her pulse quickened. She knew. She had no proof, never would have proof. But she knew. She knew who had started the ruckus.

And she knew then that she would not, could not, ask Hamilton Knapp to be the fourth member of her team.

And that is when she went to tea at Sillington House.

Margaret Draper Diamondstein must have been waiting at the window. No sooner had Mrs. Olinski stopped her van than her old friend came rushing out the door. She was wearing a jogging suit but no coat. The wind was whipping off the lake, and she hugged her upper arms and stamped her feet as she waited for the door to open. Margy Diamondstein reached up into the van, and Eva Marie Olinski reached down out of it, and they hugged.

Then a voice said, "Hi, Grandma."

It was Ethan.

Margaret asked, "Ethan? Is that you?"

"Yeah. Me. Ethan."

"Come on down out of the van and let me see you," she said. Ethan stood in front of her, looking enchantingly awkward until Margaret pulled him to her. Eva Marie Olinksi saw his arms hanging limply at his side, his wrists hanging below his cuffs like meter sticks showing how much he had grown since the jacket was new. Ethan slowly lifted his arms and fit them around his grandmother's waist as she rested her chin on the top of his head. She closed her eyes and absorbed the blond waxy smell of his hair before she stood him at arm's length. "You've grown since summer," she said.

"I have. I know," he answered, and shot his arms out of his sleeves showing several inches bare above the wrist bones. "Would you believe only a month ago, these covered my fingertips?"

Margaret laughed and said, "No, Ethan, I would not believe."

"Just testing."

Nadia waited until they had backed away from each other before saying, "Hello, Margaret."

"Nadia!" Margaret said. "What a surprise. Is Eva Marie—Mrs. Olinski—your teacher, too?"

Nadia replied, "Yes, Margaret. Yes, she is."

At that moment a slender man with heavy gray eyebrows came out of Sillington House, holding his knuckles to his hips as he looked over the scene. He saw Nadia and sprinted over, calling, "Nadia! Nadia!" He hugged her close and then kissed the top of her head several times until Ginger wedged her way between them. "I had no idea I'd see you this afternoon."

Nadia said, "Ginger is a star, Grandpa. She is excellent."

Her grandfather replied, "I have no doubt about that. After all, Ginger is a genius. And we're going to see her tomorrow night. We're all going with your mother."

"I know," Nadia said, looking very pleased. "I know."

Eva Marie Olinski watched Margaret Draper Diamondstein hug her grandson. The new Mrs. Diamondstein was dressed in a jogging suit. A turquoise jogging suit. *Turquoise!* She had always regarded the color turquoise, like shocking pink and chartreuse, as the color equivalent of the word *ain't*: quaint when seldom used but vulgar in great doses. As she watched Margaret hug her grandchild and Izzy hug his, her mental censors and her customary good manners started shutting down. She could not stand it another minute. She was on the verge of screaming with pain and rage when she felt her wheelchair begin to move. She felt herself being pushed toward the front porch of Sillington House.

Eva Marie Olinski was so blinded by jealousy that she had not noticed Mr. Singh come out. From behind her chair his voice floated down upon her in soft waves. "I have prepared a tea," he said.

A tea? She thought. Yes, a tea. It was that time of day. It was four o'clock.

"The others will join us shortly." Eva Marie Olinksi turned around and at eye level saw a long blue apron. Her eyes traveled upward and saw a black beard, a broad white smile, a pair of amber eyes, a white turban. Saved by a genie, she thought.

Mr. Singh maneuvered her wheelchair to a table in the back of the dining room. Without asking, he ceremoniously poured tea into a delicate china cup. *Cream?* No. *Sugar?* No. *Yes, it is best to drink tea without.* And she did. She drank unhurriedly. Before her cup was empty, she felt something lift from her shoulders. Was it jealousy or injury? Was it anger? Was it all the above? She replaced her emptied cup in its saucer. She waited. She was calm.

Margy and Izzy joined her at the table, and she drank another cup of tea and ate a cucumber sandwich, taking four bites out of a patch of bread so trim she could have swallowed it whole. She hardly heard what Margaret and Izzy were saying. She did not interrupt, and soon she was listening, first out of politeness—for courtesy was the first of her civilized senses to return—and then out of interest, genuine interest.

She looked around the room and saw the four children, Ethan, Noah, Nadia, and Julian sitting at a table on the far side of the room. They were talking among themselves and drinking tea. They did not interrupt one another, Mrs. Olinski thought, how unusual. There were nods and smiles and obvious pleasure in one another's company. Mrs. Olinski thought, how unusual to find four sixth graders who listen to one another sympathetically, unselfishly. How curious. How *courteous*. Mrs. Olinski thought, when people come to tea, they are courteous. She thought, I believe in courtesy. It is the way we avoid hurting people's feelings. She thought that maybe—just maybe— Western Civilization was in a decline because people did not take time to take tea at four o'clock.

The Souls continued their animated conversation, when suddenly, as if on signal, the four of them looked back at Mrs. Olinski.

And that is when she knew.

That is the exact moment she knew that Julian Singh would be the fourth member of her team and that she would always give good answers when asked why she had chosen them. And then and there, she also knew that someday she would drink another cup of slow tea at Sillington House.

Six

THE COMMISSIONER looked over his list of possible answers. "Posh and tip?" he asked. Julian quickly answered, "Posh means fashionable and is the acronym for Port Out, Starboard Home, referring to the time when India belonged to Britain, and the people traveling there wanted the shady side of the ship both going and coming. And tip, meaning the small sum of money given for services rendered, is the acronym for To Insure Promptness."

The commissioner laughed. "You may be a little ahead of us on that one, Epiphany. I don't have either of those acronyms on my list. We'll have to check with our advisory panel." He nodded to the three people sitting at a table on the far side of the room. One rapidly punched keys on a computer as the other two consulted large books. Three of them conferred briefly and passed a note to the commissioner.

"We can allow posh, but we do not find a reference for tip."

Julian said, "With all due respect, sir, I think you ought to check another source."

* * *

Their path to the state finals started with the sixth-grade championship. Mrs. Olinski had expected victory, for her team was quick and informed and worked together perfectly. No one had expected them to trounce the other two sixth grades, but they did. Their victory was so profound that the sixth-grade math teacher, Mrs. Sharkey, confided to the music teacher, Ms. Masolino, that for the first time in the history of Epiphany Middle School there was a chance—just a possibility, mind you—that a sixth-grade team might beat the seventh grade. Mrs. Sharkey said that, after all, she knew the current seventh grade, for she had taught them just last year, and in her opinion, when they were very, very good, they were mediocre.

The Souls practiced during activities hour—that portion of time between eleven-thirty and one o'clock that was not devoted to eating lunch. Mrs. Olinski read questions from note cards: one card, one question. She used three sets of questions.

The first was a series of questions required of everyone in a particular grade. Knowing that they would be competing with grade seven, she added their questions to her sixth grade set. The second set had been culled from previous contests. Some required only speed: How many quarters in twenty dollars? Some required cleverness: If one man could paint an eight foot by twelve foot wall in a half hour, how long would it take three men to paint a wall that was eight feet by twenty-four feet? The third set of questions were ones she had made up by weeding items from the news and connecting them to geography or history or both: A masterpiece by the artist Rembrandt was recently stolen from a museum in his native country. What is the country? What is its capital? Mrs. Olinski required that they find the country on a map, and then would ask them to name two other famous artists. Their countries? Their capital cities?

They beat grade seven, almost doubled their score. Fact: No sixth grade team had ever defeated a seventh grade team. They were scheduled to go up against grade eight. Further fact: No sixth grade had ever competed against the eighth because no sixth grade had ever gotten that far.

When word got out that Mrs. Olinski's homeroom had a chance of beating the eighth grade, kids from the other two sixth grades started signaling a thumbs-up sign when passing a team member in the hall. They raised their arms high overhead and lifted their thumbs like a forest of small apostrophes at the ends of their closed fists.

Excitement grew throughout the week. Mrs. Olinski's sixth graders were David versus the eighth grade Goliath, and the kids with the slingshots knew how to use them. Soon the vanquished seventh grade chose sides; they would cheer for grade six. On Thursday, the day before the showdown, kids from grades six and seven lined the halls between the cafeteria and Mrs. Olinski's room and gave her and The Souls a round of applause as they returned from lunch to practice. Mrs. Olinski smiled and said thank you, thank you as she wheeled herself between the flanks of honor guards.

Traces of her smile remained as the rest of the class filed in for social studies. She sat at her desk and sorted out the papers that were due to be returned.

The room was quiet until a student in the back of the room let out an enormous belch and said, not too sincerely, "Sorry."

Mrs. Olinski continued sorting papers before looking up. "Hamilton Knapp?"

"Yes, ma'am," he answered.

"Would you please come to the front?"

He walked slowly, watching her, a half smile on his face. She let him take his time. Before he reached the front of the classroom, someone launched another belch. Its sound rocketed forward, and the laughter that followed traveled the same trajectory. Mrs. Olinski waited until Ham reached the front of the room before asking, "Jared Lord, would you please join Mr. Knapp?"

Jared also took his time, and Mrs. Olinski did not rush him either. As he ambled down his row toward the front of the room, smiling faces lifted and tilted toward him like the broad front faces of sun-flowers as they follow the sun across heaven. Mrs. Olinski allowed that, too.

"Now, Mr. Knapp and Mr. Lord," she said, "I would like the two of you to teach the entire class how to belch on command. Please de-scribe the process for all of us." She picked up a piece of chalk from the ledge. "Which one of you wants to take notes on the instructions we are about to receive?" Neither volunteered, so she thrust the chalk into Knapp's hand. "I think you enjoy writing on the blackboard, Mr. Knapp," she said. Ham took the chalk. The class registered its ap-proval with body language that was the equivalent of silent applause.

The class waited. "I'll help you with the spelling," Mrs. Olinski said.

Ham began to clown around, rolling his eyes and saying, "Well, first you . . ."

The rest of the kids tightened their stomachs, opened their mouths, and tried to figure out how to explain a belch. Jared stood at the blackboard—empty-handed, awkward, uncomfortable—and he too, tried to figure it out. Knapp made another attempt. "Well, first you . . ." Then another long, awkward, uncomfortable wait. "Well, first you . . ."

Mrs. Olinski allowed them to stand there until three minutes seemed like thirty. Then she sent them back to their seats. "Since you cannot describe what you have done, I would call belching loudly to interrupt our class an *unspeakable act*. Unspeakable. And because you cannot explain how to do it, I would say that you cannot teach ei-ther." She paused, locked eyes first with Knapp and then with Lord before adding, "But I can. If I choose to, I can explain how to belch on command, and I could teach you. If I so choose." She looked at Knapp and Lord again, her nostrils flared slightly, then slowly turned her head to the class and added, "But I don't."

"The front of this classroom is privileged territory. There are only two reasons for you to be here. One, you are teaching something to the rest of the class, or two, you have been invited. From now on, the only tricks that I am willing to put up with are those that you can first explain and then teach."

She looked at Jared Lord and asked, "Do you understand, Mr. Lord?" Jared attempted a grin. His attempt failed, and he nodded yes. "Then let us have no more interruptions with unspeakable acts. No barking *Arf!* either. Do you understand me, Mr. Knapp?" Ham nodded yes. "Mr. Lord?" Jared said, "Yes ma'am."

As he returned to his seat, no one smiled at Ham or even made eye contact with him.

Suddenly Nadia Diamondstein thrust her left leg straight out into the aisle. Noah Gershom, who was three seats in back of her, stuck out his right leg. Ethan Potter saw and raised his right arm in the air. As if on cue, Julian Singh raised his left fist. For a moment above and below eye level, all four limbs stuck out, and then just as quickly, all four disappeared. It was quite a balancing act.

Mrs. Laurencin called a school assembly for the contest against the eighth grade. The principal herself asked the questions. If a team missed its question, the other team had an opportunity to answer. To break a tie, the last team to answer correctly had to correctly answer one additional question.

This was the question that the eighth grade could not answer and Noah could: Name all the parts of the human eye in the order that light reaches them.

This was the four part question that they answered to win: Name the famous fathers of: Queen Elizabeth I of England. Esau and Jacob. Alexander the Great. Our country.

Mrs. Laurencin was impressed. The sixth grade was jubilant. Ms. Masolino said she knew it all along, and Mrs. Sharkey said they gave new meaning to the term "bottoms up."

The Souls were now the school's team. The next step was the contest against Knightbridge for the district championship.

Seven

Any other team on spaceship Earth would have worried about Julian's defying an official of the sovereign state of New York. But not The Souls. They would let him risk whatever he wanted.

The commissioner was—to put it politely—annoyed. He looked at his seating chart. "Mr. Singh?" he asked. "Are you Julian Singh?"

"Yes, sir, I am."

"Well, Mr. Singh, we all agreed to stand by the ruling of the panel of experts."

"The panel's information is not complete, sir."

"Mr. Singh, we must stand by the ruling of the panel."

"Sir," Julian said, "long ago in England, pub owners used to place a box on the bar. They put a sign on the box that said To Insure Promptness, capitalizing each of the three words. People dropped coins . . ."

"I'll allow posh but not tip."

"With all due respect, sir, you are wrong."

At that point, the commissioner could have disqualified the entire Epiphany team—and maybe would have—except that he was rendered speechless.

* * *

To prepare for the contest with Knightsbridge, Mrs. Olinski continued to drill her team during activities hour. The week of the Knightsbridge contest, the five of them brown-bagged their lunches so that they could practice through lunch. Mrs. Olinski's packets of note cards grew. She drew questions at random from each of the three sets. The Souls had become so familiar with some of them that she had to ask only, "What did Martin Luther . . ." before four hands shot up in the air and four voices would shout out, "The Ninety-five Theses."

That would not do. Answering before a question was completed or having several kids answer at once were violations of the rules that would cost points. Mrs. Olinski reminded them that if they continued to do that, the penalties could easily add up to a loss. Her team seemed to communicate with a secret stealth language that slipped beneath thought. It took only one warning, and they stopped. Just. Like. That.

With the success of her team, Mrs. Olinski was asked more and more often how she had chosen them, and she continued to give several good answers, varying them as the need arose. They worked well together. They were willing to take time to drill. They understood the rules. They were quick. All of these answers were true, but not the whole truth. The whole truth was that Mrs. Olinski did not yet know the whole truth.

Then the day before the contest for the district championship Mr. Connor LeDue, the principal of Knightsbridge Middle School, found some pretext to visit Mrs. Olinski. He stood to one side of her wheelchair, leaned over, smiled, and said, "I heard a rumor that your team is expecting to blow mine out of the water." His smile was as genuine as a Xeroxed signature.

In order to make eye contact with someone standing where Mr. LeDue stood, Mrs. Olinski had to stretch her neck in two directions—up and to the side—and open her eyes wide. This made her look worshipful. She wasn't.

Mr. LeDue applied his smile again and said, "I told our coach that she could expect to be hung if she lets your sixth grade grunges beat us out."

"Well then," Mrs. Olinski replied, "much as I respect your coach, I recommend that you start buying rope." She shifted her head slightly and added, "By the way, Mr. LeDue, in our grunge neighborhood, we say *hanged*, not *hung*. Check it out."

Dr. Roy Clayton Rohmer, the district superintendent, was a worried man. Item one: He worried about his contract that was up for renewal. Item two: He worried about the district playoffs. Item three: He worried about Mr. Homer Fairbain, his deputy superintendent in charge of instruction. He worried because item three could affect item two, which could affect item one.

The previous year when Mr. Homer Fairbain had been master of ceremonies for the district playoffs, the contest had been broadcast on educational TV. When he was to ask the question, *What is the native country of Pope John Paul II?* Mr. Fairbain asked, "What is the native country of Pope John Paul Eye Eye?" The day after the broadcast, there were five letters to the editor in the paper about Mr. Fairbain, none favorable.

Dr. Rohmer knew that this year's broadcast would have a larger than usual audience, partly because people were curious about having a sixth grade team be a contender for the district middle school championship but mostly because everyone would be waiting for Homer Fairbain to goof. Dr. Rohmer had to let Mr. Fairbain be master of ceremonies again. It would be his one chance to show the community that he had learned a thing or II.

Dr. Rohmer knew that if the names of any of the former Soviet Socialist Republics—Uzbekistan or Azerbaijan or, Heaven forbid! Kyrgyzstan—appeared in any of the questions, Homer would embarrass himself. If he had to read the names of the ministers of Japan or Zaire, or any name containing more consonants than vowels, or more vowels than consonants, he would embarrass himself. He would also embarrass Dr. Rohmer and make him worry a lot.

Mr. Fairbain, who was a humble man, saw no problem with requesting help from one of the reading teachers until Dr. Rohmer pointed out the entire staff of remedial reading teachers came from the very department he was in charge of.

Dr. Rohmer, whose patience was as close to the end as his contract, arranged to give Mr. Fairbain the questions a week in advance, told him to practice reading them out loud and strongly suggested that if he had any difficulty with them—anything at all—to see one of the school's speech therapists. (Therapists came from the department of student services, not curriculum.)

The Souls stayed after school late the Thursday before the Knightsbridge contest. Mrs. Laurencin sent in Cokes and pizza for the team. On Friday afternoon, she came into Mrs. Olinski's room and told the team that after this practice she wanted everyone to go home and get a good night's sleep, and that win, lose, or draw, she couldn't be more proud of all of them tomorrow than she was at that moment.

For all the reasons given—an unprecedented sixth grade championship team, the snobbishness and arrogance of the Knightsbridge team, as well as waiting for Mr. Fairbain to make a fool of himself—the Knightsbridge cafetorium was filled to capacity. Small kids were perched on tabletops because there weren't enough chairs, and the Epiphany sixth graders stood like caryatids leaning against three of the four walls of the room.

Mr. Fairbain did well and actually seemed to be enjoying himself until syllabication did him in. The question was to name the tribe associated with each of the following Native American leaders and name a major accomplishment of one. The leaders' names were Sequoyah, Tecumseh, Osceola, and Geronimo. However, *Geronimo* was hyphenated at a line break, so *Gero* appeared on one line and *nimo* on the next, and unfortunately, Mr. Fairbain read it as Jair-oh-NEEM-oh.

Dr. Rohmer hoped that no one would notice and no one on the Knightsbridge team did. Fact: They could not answer the question. Then it was The Soul's turn to answer, and Julian corrected Mr. Fairbain. "With all due respect, sir, I believe one of the men of whom you speak is Geronimo, a member of the Apache tribe."

Poor Mr. Fairbain. He looked down at the card, squinted, read it, and said, "Yes, indeed, you are right, young man. Good for you." He caught Dr. Rohmer's eye and knew he had done something wrong. He laughed nervously and said, "You look a bit like an Indian yourself."

Julian smiled. "I am a hybrid. I am in part what is called East Indian."

"Well, now, that is special," Mr. Fairbain said, smiling and looking over the audience, and wanting to reinforce his compliment, asked, "What is your tribe?"

Dr. Rohmer paled to the point of translucence, and the audience gasped. Everyone—even those who had not had diversity training at taxpayer expense—knew that even though it was correct to recognize a person's ethnicity, it was not correct to comment upon it in public.

Mrs. Olinski thought Dr. Rohmer would have to be taken out on a stretcher. Mr. Fairbain noticed Dr. Rohmer's sudden anemia, and without knowing what he had done wrong, but knowing it was something, said, "That's all very interesting, young man, but I'm afraid we must move along. Can you answer the question or not?"

"I can, sir," Julian replied. And he did.

His answer put Epiphany ahead.

They had to answer one more question: What is the origin of the phrase, "to meet one's Waterloo" and what does it mean?

There was a clear, bright gleam in Ethan's eye as he concluded his answer with, ". . . *to meet one's Waterloo* means to suffer a crushing de-feat." Crushing applause followed a nanosecond of crushing silence. Everyone clapped. But not the sixth-grade sentinels who lined the walls. Instead, upon a signal from Michael Froelich, they took from their pockets a piece of rope, which they pinned on their shirts in the place where a medal would go.

When The Souls came down off the stage, they stood four abreast behind Mrs. Olinski's wheelchair and pushed her toward the back of the room where the sixth graders converged and formed a phalanx that lifted her—wheelchair and all—onto their shoulders and carried her out of the building and into the parking lot.

Two of the boys stopped short of Mrs. Olinski's van. One was Michael Froelich. He hopped on top of the other fellow's shoulders and draped a noose over the antenna of Mrs. Olinski's van.

Ethan said, "Look, Ma, no hands," and Noah said, "Look, Ma, no legs," and Nadia thought, "Sometimes people need a lift between switches," and Julian said nothing but rubbed the little ivory monkey in his pocket.

Other victories followed, but none was sweeter.

Eight

AFTER DEFEATING KNIGHTSBRIDGE, The Souls started drilling for the regionals.

There were eight regions in the state. Each was named for a major body of water that touched the counties within its boundary. They were named for lakes, great and small; for rivers, flowing south or east, and one was named for a sound, Long Island Sound. Epiphany was in the region called Finger Lakes. Finger Lakes had never won the state championship. The Hudson River region, which included Maxwell Middle School, had won three out of the past four years.

The week before the regionals, Mrs. Olinski arranged with Mrs. Laurencin to have the school opened on Saturday afternoon so they could have an extra drill. Her team had always been willing—even eager—to practice, so she was surprised and disappointed when they refused.

Finally Noah spoke. "No disrespect intended, Mrs. Olinski, but we would prefer not to."

No disrespect, but. But what? But they prefer not to! "What happens on Saturday that is more important than an extra practice session?" she asked.

Noah answered, "We have tea. On Saturdays we all have tea."

"You have *tea?*" she asked.

"Yes," Noah said. "We have tea."

"At Sillington House," Nadia added.

"At four," Ethan added.

Then Julian said, "Tea is always at four, Mrs. Olinski."

Mr. Singh's teas at Sillington House were becoming well known in the community, and Mrs. Olinski remembered her half promise to herself after the matinee of *Annie*. She would have another cup of slow tea, and the children had just extended a half invitation. Two halves make a whole, she thought. She would go to tea at Sillington House at four o'clock on Saturday afternoon.

At precisely three forty-five Mrs.Olinski locked the door to her house, got in her van, and drove to Sillington House. She arrived at four and had hardly let herself down from her van when she saw the front door swing open and Mr. Singh come down the path to the curb. He insisted upon wheeling her up the ramp across the wide porch. He paused before entered the front hall and said, "We are glad you have come, Mrs. Olinski."

"Why?" she asked.

"Because Sillington House is its own place, Mrs. Olinski. You will soon see." He wheeled her through the front hall and into the dining room where The Souls were standing behind a table in the back.

There were two other tables where paying guests were already seated. They smiled and nodded at her in the approving way people do when they see people in wheelchairs.

Mr. Singh wheeled her around to the side of the table opposite The Souls. They greeted her. Quietly. In unison. One word. They said, "Welcome." A place had been set at the end on the side table away from the wall. Handicap parking, she thought.

Julian said, "We have not yet poured your tea, Mrs. Olinski. We did not want it to get cold."

Ethan poured. Mrs. Olinski lifted her cup in a silent toast and slowly sipped. Even before replacing her cup in its saucer, she once again felt something lift from her shoulders. She nibbled on the small sandwiches with no crust and soft fillings and ate the tiny tarts with bites as delicate as the tarts themselves. Mrs. Olinski felt—the sensation was so strange to her that she hardly remembered the word—relaxed. She could not remember a time since her accident—maybe even before it—when she had not forced herself not to notice people noticing her. Yet, the children watched her eat cake and drink tea, and she did not feel at all self-conscious. Mrs. Olinski finished the last of the miniature cream puffs, delicately touched her napkin to the corners of her mouth, folded it, laid it on the table alongside her saucer, lifted her eyes, and saw four smiles adorn the faces opposite her. She returned their smiles with a grin.

Other paying guests had arrived, and The Souls excused themselves as they made trips in and out of the kitchen bringing tea and tiered trays of tea sandwiches and cakes. They rejoined Mrs. Olinski at her table, and waited until the creased V between her eyes smoothed out and disappeared altogether. Then when the last of the paying guests had paid his check, Noah said, "We begin practice after we clear up."

There was a tip under the rim of the saucer on each of the tables of the paying guests. Whoever picked up the money put it into a box on the sideboard to which a small sign, written in calligraphy said, TO IN-SURE PROMPTNESS.

After The Souls had disappeared into the kitchen, Mr. Singh came out. He laid several packs of note cards on the table and sat across the table from Mrs. Olinski. He sat with his back as straight as his chair, and said, "They were getting worried, Mrs. Olinski."

"Who was?"

"The Souls, Mrs. Olinski."

"The Souls?" she repeated. "Who are The Souls?"

"It would be more proper to ask, *what* are The Souls."

"All right, then. *What* are The Souls?"

"The Souls, Mrs. Olinski, are what Noah, Nadia, Ethan, and Julian have become. Do you understand?"

"No, Mr. Singh, I'm afraid I don't. Is this some strange Indian philosophy, Mr. Singh? Reincarnation. That sort of thing?"

He smiled. His smile was as white as his turban and almost as broad. "An incarnation, perhaps. Not a reincarnation. Nadia chose the name."

"Why were they getting worried?"

"They worried, Mrs. Olinski, because you were on the verge of choosing another. Such a choice would have been disastrous."

Mrs. Olinski had never told anyone—*anyone*—that she had been on the verge of choosing another. She grew uneasy. Why was Mr. Singh destroying the wonderful relaxed feeling she had had only minutes ago? She nervously cleared her throat. "But I did not," she said defensively.

"Yes. It was most fortunate. They have been waiting, Mrs. Olinski."

She said, "I'm afraid I still don't understand. Waiting for what? What are you trying to tell me, Mr. Singh?"

He smiled. The white of his teeth made a dazzling underline to his turban. "Just think about this, will you? You have never been able to explain how you chose the members of your team. You have given an-swers but no explanations."

How did he know that?

"Think of the atom, Mrs. Olinski. There are energies within that tiny realm that are invisible but produce visible results." Mr. Singh shook his head slowly. "Do not feel uneasy, Mrs. Olinski. Hamilton Knapp would truly have been a terrible choice."

Mrs. Olinski had never told anyone—*anyone*—that she had been on the verge of choosing Hamilton Knapp. How could Mr. Singh tell her not to be uneasy when everything he said made her uneasy!

Mr. Singh stood. "Later," he said. "Later you will understand. But for now, we would like to express our gratitude for realizing that Julian was the necessary soul."

She nodded. "All right," she said. "Later."

He pushed the packets of cards in front of her. "Would you like to be quizmaster today?"

"I guess I would."

"I'll send them in. They are ready to begin."

She absentmindedly turned over the cards. There was one question per card, just like hers, but these were written, not typed. The writing was calligraphic, the paper white, the ink as black as Hecate's soul. She examined the questions—they were good ones—and hardly noticed when the children had come out of the kitchen and taken places at the table on the side opposite her.

"Who wrote these?" she asked.

Noah said, "We all did. I gave Julian a calligraphy kit for our first Saturday, and I taught them all."

"Who made up the questions?"

"You made up some," Julian said. "And the rest of us contributed others."

"You, too, Mr. Singh?"

Mr. Singh bowed slightly from the waist. "My specialties are languages and weights and measures. Cooks must know weights and measures."

Mrs. Olinski laughed. "Where did you come up with that category?"

"I'm a big fan of *Jeopardy!* on the television. When Julian and I lived on the cruise ship, they very often had quiz contests to amuse the patrons. This happened very often when the weather was bad." He bowed again. "If you will be quizmaster today, Mrs. Olinski, I shall return to my kitchen. I am trying out new recipes for bran muffins. Americans care very much for bran. I learned of this when I was on the cruise ship." He smiled. "We must talk again, Mrs. Olinski."

Noah was saying, "There are some holes we need to plug, Mrs. Olinski."

"What are they?" she asked.

Julian answered. "Music and the Bible."

Noah said, "I keep telling Julian that we can skip the Bible."

Julian said, "When I watch *Jeopardy!* with Papa, the Bible is very often a category. I think we need it."

Noah said, "Fact: This is New York. Not India, not England, and certainly not a cruise ship. This is New York. And fact: There is the law. There is no way anyone involved with teaching in a public school in the state of New York is going to quiz anyone who is in school at taxpayer expense on the Bible. They'd be slapped with fourteen lawsuits before the buzzer finished sounding. Don't you agree that's a fact, Mrs. Olinski?"

Mrs. Olinski was not thinking about the facts. She was thinking about their name, The Souls. "I like it," she said out loud.

"You like the Bible?"

"Well, yes," she replied. "I like the Bible. As literature, as history, I'm comfortable with it as a category."

Noah sighed. "Does that mean the New Testament and the Old Testament?"

"Wouldn't hurt," Mrs. Olinski replied.

"And the Koran?"

"Wouldn't hurt," Mrs. Olinski replied.

"The Upanishads?" Julian asked.

"Those, too?" Noah asked.

"Wouldn't hurt," they all said in unison. And then they all laughed until Noah caught on and laughed, too.

It was dark when Mrs. Olinski left Sillington House, and she was glad. The dark wrapped the afternoon around her and kept it close. Sillington House was its own place. She lifted one hand from the steering wheel, whipped it off to one side, and snapped her fingers. She laughed. The Finger Lakes Regional Championship was in the bag.

Nine

THE COMMISSIONER OF EDUCATION, recovered from the shock of having a contestant protest a ruling, cited Julian. He took away the two points he had been given for answering half of the question and gave Maxwell a chance to answer. The two acronyms they gave were MADD: Mothers Against Drunk Driving. Julian was about to protest that answer on the basis that MADD was not a true acronym because it was a word even before it became an acronym. But the word itself was spelled with one *d* not two, so Julian, who was patient beyond his years, said nothing and waited. Maxwell next came up with SONAR.

While waiting for them to decide what sonar stood for, one of the panel of experts looked up from a heavy volume and sent a signal to the commissioner. He walked over to her. When he returned to the lectern, he said, "We have an adjustment to make on the score. Tip is an acronym for To Insure Promptness. We restore the five points we subtracted as penalty and add four for answering the question. Maxwell will be allowed to retain two points for MADD but will not receive credit for SONAR."

Julian said, "Thank you, sir."

No one dared applaud, but everyone in the row to the left of Mrs. Olinski sported smiles that were very loud, and in the row behind her, Nate and Sadie, Izzy and Margy sat on their hands. Even Margy got that excited.

* * *

Between their regional championship and their trip to Albany, word had gotten out that something unusual was happening in Epiphany. Mrs. Laurecin had made a call to the local newspaper, and Mrs. Olinski and The Souls were featured above the fold on the first page of the metro section of the Epiphany *Times*.

That started the blitz of publicity to which Dr. Roy Clayton Rohmer happily surrendered. He hungered for "positive taxpayer feedback," so he called a press conference. After Holly Blackwell, the popular anchorwoman of Channel Three Eyewitness News, accepted his invitation, he invited Mrs. Olinski, The Souls, Mrs. Laurencin, and Mr. Homer Fairbain to attend.

While arranging The Souls behind Dr. Rohmer like a backdrop of the American flag, Holly Blackwell pointed the microphone at Nadia and, pitching her voice a full octave higher than her on-air voice, asked, "And * where * did * we * get * all * these * bee-YOU-tee-ful * red * curls?"

Nadia looked around. "We?" she asked. "Does someone else have red hair?" Whereupon Holly Blackwell turned her back on all The Souls and instructed the cameraman to pan across their faces occasionally but to focus on Dr. Rohmer. Mrs. Olinski was not pleased. Here were four kids who could speak in complete sentences without a single *you-know* as filler, and Holly Blackwell asked them nothing. She asked Mrs. Olinski one question. Guess what it was. How did she choose her team? Mrs. Olinski gave one of her good answers: her "complementary skills" response, dressing it up to say that the team's talents blended like a chorus, making one sound of many voices. But her answer ended up on the cutting room floor.

Dr. Homer Fairbain was under orders to smile a lot and say nothing except, "The taxpayers are very proud." He asked Dr. Rohmer if he could say, "We are very proud of these youngsters." No. Just "The taxpayers are very proud." How about, "Everyone is very proud of this team?" No. Just "The taxpayers are very proud." And smile. Smile for Holly, the camera, and the sake of ed-you-kay-shun.

So the session was almost over when Holly Blackwell tilted her coif and turned her baby-blues on the deputy superintendent and asked him how the trip to Albany would be financed. Homer Fairbain smiled and replied, "The taxpayers are very proud." Dr. Rohmer grew as pale as the paper of his unsigned contract.

Having followed orders, Mr. Fairbain provided the only real news that came out of the news conference. Mrs. Laurencin immediately called the school bus dispatcher and reserved six big yellow ones to take the Epiphany boosters to Albany.

Dr. Rohmer said that the taxpayers were proud but not that proud. He said that unlike football matches where he could charge admission to the games, there was no precedent for charging admission to the Academic Bowl. Taxpayer money would pay Mrs. Olinski's expenses and The Souls', would even pay Mrs. Laurencin's and, of course, his own, but he would not, could not, pay for chartered buses to take the entire town of Epiphany to Albany. He would allow the buses to be used, but he would not pay for the gas or the driver.

And that was when Century Village came through.

Noah's mother had taped the press conference and sent it to Noah's Grandma Sadie and Grandpa Nate who, in turn, shared it with everyone in the clubhouse at Century Village. They commissioned Bella Dubinsky to design a T-shirt. At the suggestion of Mrs. Froelich, she drew a noose. Nothing else. Sadie Gershom suggested that she put the name of the school under that.

Bella refused. "Less is more," she said.

"Not if it's wins over losses," Sadie answered.

But she liked the design, after all, and they arranged to have it silk screened on five hundred red T-shirts, which they shipped north. They sold for ten dollars apiece, and the profit paid for the gas for the buses. The drivers donated their services.

Mrs. Olinski drove to Albany, taking Julian and Mr. Singh with her.

Ten

THE JUDGES ADJUSTED THE SCORE for the acronym question, which put Epiphany ahead. Then Maxwell answered: Who was the first president to live in the White House? and the score was even. Then Epiphany answered: What is the waste product of photosynthesis? Maxwell named the three major food groups, and Epiphany answered, "Who was the first Spanish explorer to reach Florida?" The lead ping-ponged back and forth as the teams took turns answering.

* * *

Mr. Singh said, "You are a very good driver, Mrs. Olinski." The rhythm of his speech was something between a chant and a birdcall. "I have not myself a high degree of skill for driving automobiles. For many years we lived on a cruise ship, and so I was a fully mature man before I passed my first driving test. Did you require many lessons to learn to drive a handicapped vehicle?"

"I had a few," Mrs. Olinski replied. They rode in silence, listening only to the muffled thump and whirr of the tires riding over the interstate before Mrs. Olinski added, "After my accident it took more courage to get back into the passenger's side of an automobile than it took for me to learn to drive again."

"I can understand that," Mr. Singh replied. "It often takes more courage to be a passenger than a driver. Of course, Mrs. Olinski, I am in no way making reference to this trip."

Julian sat alone in the back seat and read the trees and houses and road signs. He said almost nothing, but Mrs. Olinski was never not aware of him. Finally, she said, "Julian makes each mile a journey of quarter inches."

Mr. Singh replied, "It is a skill he learned when we lived on the cruise ship, Mrs. Olinski. He learned to be a passenger. He learned to read the ocean by the cupful. He also learned to regard each port of call as part of the journey and not as destination. Every voyage begins when you do."

"When you fill your pen," Mrs. Olinski said.

Mr. Singh smiled. "Yes, Noah told us."

Suspense grew, and the commissioner did his best to sustain it. He took his time between questions. He looked over at the judges, nodded, reached into the bowl, and slowly, slowly unfolded the paper. "This question is Maxwell's." Everyone knew that Maxwell would have to answer correctly to tie it up again. The commissioner tugged ever so gently at his French cuff. He adjusted his glasses. He cleared his throat. He read, "In what work of fiction would we meet the original Humpty Dumpty, and who wrote it?"

The answer came. "*Alice's Adventures in Wonderland* by . . ."

"No!" said the commissioner of education before they could supply an answer to the second part and throw the judges into a panic about the possibility of having to award Maxwell half credit and create confusion about the score.

There was an audible gasp from the audience. Didn't they all believe—those who had actually read *Alice* and not just said they had—that Humpty Dumpty came from Wonderland? Behind her Mrs. Olinski heard Grandpa Nate Gershom whisper to Grandma Sadie, "I think it's Mother Goose. Logic tells me that an egg would come from a mother and a goose."

The commissioner of education tapped on his microphone and demanded quiet. While the audience waited, he took his Mark Cross pen from his inside jacket pocket and wrote on the back of the question in question: To be discussed: The use of compound questions for match point. He replaced his pen in his inside jacket pocket, turned to his right and asked, "Epiphany, can you answer?"

Nadia, Noah, and Ethan looked at Julian, inviting him to give the correct answer. "*Through the Looking Glass* by Lewis Carroll."

It was match point. Epiphany must answer a follow-up to be declared the winner. The commissioner looked again at the paper in his hand. Several spaces beneath and printed in italics was the follow-up: *What was the true name and occupation of the author?* Julian knew: Reverend Charles Lutwidge Dodgson; math teacher, Oxford University.

It was over.

* * *

Between reality and realization, there was a pause. It was over. There was a beat—time for hearts to skip. There was a gap—time for hearts and minds to connect. There was a moment for joy to find its home. It was over. And Epiphany had won.

The Maxwell side of the room was the first to clap. Epiphany, the first to cheer.

The team from Maxwell walked over to The Souls, shook their hands as they had been taught to do, and smiled the parched way that losers do.

The Souls smiled triumphantly. At the audience and for the cameras. There must have been a hundred cameras flashing and whirring. With spots dancing in their eyes, they walked to the edge of the small stage and stood in front of Mrs. Olinski and applauded her specifically until everyone else got the message and stood and faced her and applauded her, too. Mrs. Olinski smiled and said thank you and smiled and nodded and said thank you, thank you, over and over again, wheeling her chair in small circles until her smile and her words floated like a frieze around the room.

The Souls came down from the stage then and, two by two, stood on either side of her wheelchair, so the commissioner had to come down off stage to give them their trophy. They didn't want it unless Mrs. Olinski was there with them.

And The Souls and Mrs. Olinski shared the trophy that is called a loving cup. And it was.

And then it was all over.

Eleven

THEY HAD NO SOONER made it to the interstate than Julian fell asleep.

Mrs. Olinski and Mr. Singh were quiet, too. Mrs. Olinski felt a strange sense of loss. She did not feel like a loser, but she did feel a sense of loss. She drove for miles worrying about it. Finally, almost involuntarily, she said out loud, "Win some. Lose some." She glanced at Mr. Singh and laughed. "Why did I say that?"

Mr. Singh replied, "Because it is how you feel at this moment, Mrs. Olinski."

"I am happy that we won, Mr. Singh. But I don't understand why I feel a sense of loss. This is not like my accident when my loss was overwhelming. Why, after this wonderful victory, do I feel that something is missing?"

"Because something is." Miles hummed past before his voice floated back to her. "For many months now, you have been in a state of perpetual preparation and excitement. Each victory was a preparation for the next. You are missing future victories. Have you enjoyed the journey out, Mrs. Olinski?"

"Very much. Every cupful. Like Julian on the ocean."

"Now, you must put down anchor, look around, enjoy this port of call. Your stay will be brief. You must do it, Mrs. Olinski."

Julian did not wake up even when they stopped for gas in Oneonta. He had stretched out in the back, and the bright lights of the service station shone through the rear window. His lips were slightly parted. His eyelashes cast semicircles of shadow on his cheeks.

"What do you see, Mrs. Olinski?" Mr. Singh asked.

"I see that angels have landed on his eyelids."

"Yes," he answered, pleased. "Angels have."

A car pulled in behind Mrs. Olinski. Its lights hit her rearview mirror, which she adjusted and then said abruptly, "Mr. Singh, do you know how I chose The Souls?"

Mr. Singh laughed. "I believe you have several good answers.

Which would you like?"

"I am not asking for my answers, Mr. Singh. I am asking for yours."

Mr. Singh replied, "The Souls have all returned from a journey, Mrs. Olinski."

"A journey, Mr. Singh? All of them?"

"Yes. Each of them. Noah was first."

"Well, yes, he was the first chosen."

"And the first to return from his journey. From Century Village."

"Nadia?"

"From the Sargasso Sea."

"Ethan?"

"Ethan took a little longer than the other two, yet his journey was the shortest. It was a ride on the school bus."

"And Julian was last."

"Yes. Julian was last. His journey has been the longest."

Mr. Singh said nothing more. Mrs. Olinski drove past several exits on the interstate, waiting. As they approached the ramp that would take them to the state highway that would lead to Epiphany, he had still said nothing. She could stand it no longer. "Mr. Singh," she demanded, "you must finish. You must tell me what you know about their journeys."

"They found something, Mrs. Olinski. Noah at Century Village; Nadia on the Sargasso Sea; Ethan on the bus." He hesitated. "Think about the question that Maxwell missed. They did not know that Humpty Dumpty was not in Wonderland because they never journeyed through the looking glass to find him. How can you know what is missing if you've never met it? You must know of something's existence before you can notice its absence. So it was with The Souls. They found on their journeys what you found at Sillington House."

"A cup of kindness, Mr. Singh? Is that what I found?"

"Kindness, yes, Mrs. Olinski. Noah, Nadia, and Ethan found kindness in others and learned how to look for it in themselves. Can you know excellence if you've never seen it? Can you know good if you have seen only bad? Julian knows—perhaps even more than the others—about kindness. We have, my son and I, been most fortunate. We have found much kindness when we journeyed on the ship. When sixth grade started, my son found malice. Spite and malice. Mean things were done to him. Julian has told me many stories. Many stories." The music of his voice faded and stopped. He looked at, not through, the windshield as if it were a small screen showing one of the many stories, and then back in focus, he said to Mrs. Olinski, "Each of The Souls has had a journey, and so have you, Mrs. Olinski."

Eva Marie Olinski thought back to the day she had chosen Julian. That was the day she did not choose Hamilton Knapp. She had seen something as she scanned the rows in the auditorium. Something that made her not choose him. She had seen how mean he was, and that was the day she went to tea at Sillington House.

They were riding down Gramercy Road now, and Mr. Singh started to turn toward the back of the van to awaken Julian. He stopped and quietly asked, "Do you know, Mrs. Olinski, how Julian first invited The Souls to tea?"

"How?"

"He sent them invitations hidden in a book."

"What book might that be, Mr. Singh?"

"The book was *Alice's Adventures in Wonderland*. He would never make the mistake of looking for Humpty Dumpty there."

They said nothing more except good night.

As tired as she was, Mrs. Olinski took her copy of *Alice's Adventures in Wonderland* down from the shelf. She found the Cheshire Cat but no Humpty Dumpty. As Mr. Singh had said, if you've not seen something, it's hard to know what is missing. She took down *Through the Looking Glass* and found Humpty Dumpty sitting on a wall.

> *Humpty Dumpty had a great fall.*
> *All the King's horses and all the King's men*
> *Couldn't put Humpty Dumpty in his place again.*

All the king's horses and all the king's men could not have done for Mrs. Eva Marie Olinski what the kindness of four sixth-grade souls had.

She closed her book, put it back on the shelf together again with *Alice's Adventures in Wonderland*. She went to bed with a grin, which like the Cheshire Cat's, remained for some time after. For a considerable time after.

Twelve

Eva Marie Olinski let herself down out of her van and wheeled herself to the bottom of the front porch ramp of Sillington House. The Souls were waiting. They opened the front door for her.

And that is when she knew that they knew that she knew.

They made their way to the big familiar table in the back of the dining room.

Mr. Singh had opened the windows along the side wall, and a breeze from the lake breathed sweet spring air into the room. At last the weather had caught up with the calendar. Then Mr. Singh took a seat opposite her at the far end of the table. She waited until they were all in their usual places, and then she asked, "Did I choose you, or did you choose me?"

And The Souls answered, "Yes!"

Fifteen Questions with Thirty-Six Answers

What is the meaning of the word *calligraphy* and from what language does it derive?

Calligraphy derives from Greek.
It means beautiful writing.

What is the name given to the portion of the North Atlantic Ocean that is noted for its abundance of seaweed, and what is its importance to the ecology of our planet?

The Sargasso Sea.
Its relatively still waters and its abundance of seaweed allow many species of marine animals to feed and grow.

What famous American women are associated with the following places in New York State and why are they important?

Seneca Falls

Elizabeth Cady Stanton.
Called the first women's rights conventions here in 1848.

Homer

Amelia Jenks Bloomer.
Was born here. Was editor of Lily, a paper devoted to women's rights and temperance. She wore a short skirt and full trousers whenever she lectured, and they became known as the Bloomer costume or bloomers.

Rochester

> Susan B. Anthony.
> *Led a group of women to the polls here in 1872 to test the right of women to vote. She was arrested, tried, and sentenced to a fine.*

Auburn

> Harriet Tubman.
> *One of the most successful conductors of the underground railroad, she lived here for many years.*

How many quarters in twenty dollars?
> *Eighty*

If one man can paint an eight feet by twelve feet wall in a half hour, how long would it take three men to paint a wall that is eight feet by twenty-four feet?
> *Twenty minutes*

A masterpiece by the artist Rembrandt was recently stolen from a museum in his native country. What is the country?
> *The Netherlands*

What is the capital?
> *Amsterdam*

Name the parts of the human eye in the order that light reaches them.
> *Cornea, aqueous humor, pupil of iris, vitreous humor, retina*

Name the famous fathers of :

Queen Elizabeth I of England

> *King Henry VIII*

Esau and Jacob

> *Isaac*

Alexander the Great

> *Philip of Macedon*

Our country

George Washington

Name the tribe associated with each of the following Native
American leaders and name a major accomplishment of one.

Sequoyah

Cherokee.
Created a system for writing the Cherokee language; the giant tree,
sequoia, is named for him.

Tecumseh

Shawnee.
Great organizer and leader, was made a brigadier general by the
British in the War of 1812.

Osceola

Seminole.
Resisted the removal of Native Americans to the West.

Geronimo

Apache.
Led a group of followers into Mexico resisting resettlement of his
group to an arid reservation.

What is the origin of the phrase "to meet one's Waterloo" and what
does it mean?
Napoleon's last battle was at Waterloo in Belgium. He was defeated by
the Duke of Wellington in 1815.
To meet one's Waterloo means to suffer a resounding defeat.

What is SONAR an acronym for?
SOund NAvigation Ranging: using sound waves for locating
submerged objects and for communication with submarines.

Who was the first president to live in the White House?
John Adams

What is the waste product of photosynthesis?
  Oxygen

Name the three major food groups.
  Proteins, carbohydrates, fats

Who was the first Spanish explorer to reach Florida?
  Ponce de León

Related Readings

Joyce Hansen

A Safe Space

Like the students in The View from Saturday, *Tommy knows that he is different from most other students in his school. He identifies himself as a "closet brainiac" and finds some very good friends with whom to share the title.*

CONCENTRATE! Only one hour before showtime, people," Mr. Walker yells. "You're out of sync, son. Stand still. Don't move." A few people giggle. We know who he's shouting at as he taps his baton on the podium.

Poor Tommy. His voice wasn't bad, deep bass like mine. But he couldn't move in time to the music. I knew he shouldn't have joined our high school gospel chorus. I tried to talk him out of it. But like my girlfriend Deidre always says, "Tommy's been around us so long he don't know he's white anymore."

Walker is springing up and down and waving his arms. Tommy stands next to me and I feel him twitch when the altos and sopranos begin to sing "I'll Fly Away," his favorite. And I know that by the time the tenors and the bass join in he will move even though Walker told him not to because Tommy is a feeling person. And the music moves you. It was just that Tommy didn't move the way the rest of us did. For some of our songs we sway from side to side as we sing. Walker is a perfectionist. I call him Perfect Pitch. "We move as one body. We sing with one voice, people," he'd shout at us.

It's our turn. As the tenors and bass sing I can't look at Tommy and he can't keep still. If I look at him I'll get out of whack too. "Concentrate," Walker shouted again. "We move as one body." I wish I could help Tommy.

"*I'll fly away oh glory, I'll fly away.*" Tommy sings with all of his heart. Happy. He breaks loose and moves to his own time. Doesn't care what anyone thinks. Not like me. I've tried to be like Tommy. Not caring. It doesn't work for me. But Tommy never worries about what people think of him. He's been that way ever since I first met him.

The first thing I noticed about Tommy when he walked into the auditorium at freshman orientation two years ago was his large round face and dirty blond hair that wouldn't settle down on his head. *Moonface*. The fact that he was the only white student in the entire ninth grade made him stand out even more—like a big white sore thumb.

I stand out too, but for different reasons—people who like me, mostly my family, call me a "big husky guy." Everyone else, especially my peers, call me *Fat Boy*. At least my size keeps people away from me until they learn that I'm not a fighter. I am just a boy who likes to stay to himself.

On freshman day as I watched kids streaming into the auditorium I scanned the room for a familiar face from my old junior high school—not that it mattered. I had no friends in junior high school anyway. Instead of seeing a familiar face, I saw Tommy, a very new face. I figured that he wouldn't last a week, and wondered why he was attending Lincoln High School. There were only a handful of white students in the school and they were all seniors. My mom called them the remnants—the families who never left the neighborhood once it changed. "Too poor to leave." She knows everything. I wonder whether she knows why my father left us.

Ninth graders continued to drift into the auditorium and I saw a few familiar faces from junior high school. It didn't take me long to guess who was who and what was what.

The athletes were tall, loud and handsome. Then there were the boys who weren't athletes and they weren't handsome either, but the girls liked them anyway. They knew how to tease girls and put their arms around them without getting slapped upside the head, and they knew how to walk down the hall sideways and make girls laugh. I love girls too, but I am not what the old folks call "a ladies' man."

And there were the boys like me—closet brainiacs. I tried to see if I could recognize any more of us. It was hard, though, because we hide. Some of us hide behind silly grins and others behind bad attitudes. And some, like me, try to disappear completely.

I checked out the girls next. A few of them looked shy and mousy and seemed like they were afraid. Others were boisterous as hell, acting like they were still in junior high school. Next I checked out the fly, pretty girls who God made just for the athletes. Then there was one girl who stood out from the rest. *The Most Popular Girl in the World*.

I noticed her only because she seemed to know everyone. She was thin, small and dark and wasn't much to write home about, I thought, mostly because she was easy to miss in a crowd of athletes and fly girls.

I don't think any of us noticed too much after we left the auditorium, because as soon as we entered the hallway where the real jocks and players ruled, we were little no-counts and nerds who didn't matter in the great scheme of things. We spun in a whirlwind of students, noise and confusion. Someone yelled get those toddlers. A freshman day ritual.

Me, *Moonface* and *The Most Popular Girl in the World* bumped into one another as we tried to find our way among the stampeding students.

"Hey, I'm sorry man." Moonface ran into me. "You know where room 211 is?"

"I'm near you, room 212," a girl's voice answered.

I turned around and saw *The Most Popular Girl in the World*. I towered over her.

"I'm in room 218," I said, staring at my program. The girl's smile dazzled me, so I looked away.

She put out her hand, "My name is Deidre."

"I'm Lamont," I said.

Moonface held out his hand. "I'm Tommy."

We found our rooms together, but I didn't see them for the next two weeks. I guessed that *The Most Popular Girl in the World* was too busy with all of the people she knew, and that *Moonface* probably had transferred to the predominantly white high school on the other side of town. I was busy surviving. You could survive if you knew how. You had to do things like eat lunch quickly in a quiet corner of the cafeteria, if there was one, and then escape to the library. Instead of riding the school bus or the public buses that many of the kids used, I walked the ten blocks to my house—taking the short cut through Garvey Park.

By the second week of school everyone was settling into their places and we could sign up for extracurricular activities. Nothing interested me, but my mother bugged me about joining a school club. One morning before I left for school, we had one of our usual arguments.

"You need to join a club in your school. You spend too much time alone, Lamont."

"I like to be alone," I said, knowing that this would bring on the "Black People Are Not Loners" speech. "It's unnatural, especially for a black person. Most black people are social."

"But I'm not most black people," I said. "How do you know how most black people are, anyway?" I asked, knowing that this would bring on the "You Are Just Like Your Father" speech. I left the house before she dipped into her bag of speeches and pulled out another one.

Why couldn't she understand that being a loner wasn't such a terrible thing? Especially when you liked to write poetry. But no one knew this about me—not even my mother, or my father when he lived with us. He probably would've said that writing poetry wasn't a very manly thing to do. In his world only athletes were manly. So, I joined the writing club. Sitting quietly in a corner and writing sounded good to me. I'd stay long enough to keep my Mom quiet, then I'd go back to being my unnatural self.

When I walked into the classroom for the first meeting, who do I see but *Moonface* and *The Most Popular Girl in the World*. Deidre and Tommy sat together at a large round table. They both grinned and motioned me over to them. They acted like they'd been waiting for me. I had no choice but to sit with them.

I was annoyed, though. I figured Tommy just wanted to goof off or he was afraid of the general population and thought that the kids in the creative writing club wouldn't harrass him. And I figured Deidre liked some boy in the club, though there were not too many of us except for a table full of the guys who knew how to make girls laugh and an athlete who must've been hiding out from the real thugs who were majoring in gangsterism 101 and wanted to kick him.

Mrs. Mackey, the teacher who ran the club, reminded me of a hippie back in the sixties. Old and young at the same time.

"All of you have something important to say. Search your own hearts and minds. Everything you need to create is right here." She placed her hand on her heart. "No one is wrong here. We're exploring and creating together."

Then we did what she called a freewriting exercise. "Don't edit yourself. Be free. What you have to say is important because you're important. Find the quiet place, the safe space inside you. There has to be a place where you find peace, love and freedom from your fears. You have to find a safe space that allows you to be strong and to soar." Her voice rose. "Write, don't stop. You can't be wrong or sound stupid." Her silver earrings danced and dangled around the sides of her face as she talked. "Believe in yourself. Trust your voice, your heart."

Tommy pulled a big looseleaf notebook out of his backpack like it was special for the occasion. And he began to write and I wondered why he wrote so fast and furiously. I didn't know what to write. As a matter of fact, I thought that the whole exercise was stupid. Write anything that comes to your mind? Mrs. Hippie had talked about a safe space.

> *Mama, Papa*
> *Once a safe space in*
> *a boy's life. When did it start?*
> *Muffled sounds in the night.*
> *Cries you can't hide.*
> *The hate seeping into the cracks of the walls*
> *oozing out of ceilings sliding under doors.*

I stopped, even though she said to keep writing. I glanced at Tommy, who had written two full pages. Deidre had either drawn something, or created her own alphabet.

"Now I want us to share," Mrs. Mackey said after ten minutes, "but only if you wish to."

Everyone looked everywhere but at the teacher. No one wanted to stand up and read the crap they'd written. Then Tommy raised his big white hand. *Why?* I thought. *Why would you open yourself to ridicule?*

Tommy cleared his throat and I heard some snickers. They're going to make chicken liver out of this kid I thought to myself. He began to read and Mrs. Hippie's face grew long and stern as she gazed around the room. Giggles grew like humming insects on a hot summer day. But Tommy kept reading. He read some kind of sci fi story about an alien on another planet, and I wondered was he writing about himself and us? Suddenly the snickering stopped and we all listened to his wild story of lost worlds. This kid has seen one Star Trek episode too many, I said to myself.

But when he stopped reading just before his character is about to be crushed by a crazed robot, and announced, "I didn't finish yet," everyone groaned.

Then the athletic-looking kid says to Tommy in a deep voice that could be considered threatening if you were the scary type, "Man, don't leave me hanging like that. Finish the story the next time."

Deidre laughed and it sounded like a song. "I'll help you finish the story," she offered. "I have some ideas." Then she turned to me. "What did you write?"

"Nothing," I said.

Her smile brushed my face, like soft hands. "I bet you're a real good writer, Lamont."

I let her read it. "Don't show anyone else," I said. I don't even know what made me show her. Her smile, I suppose. I had never let anyone read my poetry except a few teachers who promised not to make me read before the class.

Tommy leaned over Deidre's shoulder. "Can I read it too?"

I figured if he had the nerve to stand up in front of us like that, then I could let him read what I'd written. It was just an exercise, anyhow. But that was the beginning of our friendship. The three of us became best buddies and Deidre ended up being my girl.

Deidre wasn't *The Most Popular Girl in the World.* That was her way of surviving and keeping people off guard. Making them think that they knew her—always helpful. She's a brainiac too. She knew she couldn't fit in with the cheerleaders, or the fly girls, and the mousy girls were boring. She really wanted to be in a math club, but Lincoln High School has no math club. So she joined the writing club, and decided to stay because she liked me. (Is the girl crazy?) She never had a boyfriend and confessed to me that most boys frightened her.

Tommy turned out to be a brainiac too. He survived so well he doesn't stand out anymore and refused to go to the white school when his father wanted to transfer him out of Lincoln. He is totally and completely unself-conscious. Impervious to ridicule. Determined to fit in. And he does. He's not the big white kid anymore, but merely Tommy.

Our writing group shrunk. Those of us who stayed really like Mrs. Mackey, even me, who isn't easy to please. She's one of the few adults I ever met who treated you like a person and not a lump of clay to change and mold in their image. The athlete remained—said he wanted to hear the end of Tommy's story. Tommy said he was creating a sci fi soap opera. And Mrs. Mackey said that a story isn't finished until it's finished. And she'd tell Deidre that it was okay to visualize her stories through drawing. She let the boys who knew how to make girls laugh create rapping, rhyming stories. And she accepted me.

"I wish you would share what you write with the other students, Lamont. It would help them, because I know that they have the same feelings. You have so much talent." Then she'd smile. "But I understand if you don't wish to read before the group." The other day I showed her "A Safe Space." I keep fooling around with it. Adding things, taking things away. I showed her a few lines that I'd added to it.

> *You know everything,*
> *yet couldn't make him stay?*
> *And You. Did you have to leave?*
> *Do you detest the sight of me and her?*
> *Is that why you hide?*
> *But you filled the house and*
> *made it a home too.*

Mrs. Mackey clasped her hands to her chest and almost looked teary-eyed. "You have a poet's soul. This is so moving."

"I'm not finished with it," I said. And left it at that.

Each time I went to the club I promised myself that I'd read in front of the class. As I tried to raise my head and my hand I'd break out in a cold sweat, then I'd feel like I was blowing up like a helium balloon. I couldn't do it.

I write stories and plays too, and I've come up with some pretty good rhymes also, but my deepest feelings can only be expressed in a poem. Mrs. Mackey always shows us different forms of writing, so we'd try new things.

I still only share what I write with Mrs. Mackey, Tommy, and Deidre. Deidre has offered to read my poems to the rest of the group, but I won't let her. I joined the gospel chorus because I thought it would help me. But it's not the same as standing alone. In the chorus, I am one of thirty people.

I feel so ridiculous because I still can't bear to hear my words read aloud. Yet, last week I did something real crazy. Mrs. Mackey is always telling me how moving my words are. Pumping me up. My mother had been bugging me all last week, telling me to let my father know about the concert. "Did you tell *your father* about the concert?"

"Yes."

"What did he say?"

"I don't know what he said."

"You act just like *your father*." She shook her head. "You can't go through life sticking to yourself like that. You can't talk to your own father? It ain't natural."

I played with her words:

> She misses you, but never speaks your name,
> or tells me why you left us alone.
> Your name is now, "Your Father."
> Your Father hasn't called.
> Your Father doesn't care.
> You act just like Your Father.

I didn't answer her because I don't think she wanted an answer. I wonder what she would say if she knew I sent him "A Safe Space" along with a note: *I'll be singing at a concert in the high school auditorium on Wednesday night at 7:30. Lamont.*

I'm wondering how I had the nerve to do that? Anger? Maybe. Spite? Maybe. If my poetry is so moving perhaps it will move him to show up at the concert tonight.

As I stand with the others and watch people strolling into the auditorium I begin to feel nervous. Then I feel anger creeping up in me as I see more and more parents, especially fathers. He won't come and he'll call me a big sissy for sitting around writing poems instead of getting out on a football field. I let Mrs. Mackey turn my head. I let her pump me up for two years and ended up doing a stupid thing like sending a poem to my father. A man of few words. I can't believe I did that.

Mr. Walker bangs the baton startling me. "People, the time is drawing nigh. Get it together, Mr. Tommy, I told you not to move. Concentrate."

Tommy wipes his forehead. "But, Mr. Walker, I didn't know I was moving."

He pulls Tommy to the side and talks with him privately, so we take a break.

Deidre walks over to me. "Lamont, we have to help him."

I have my own problems. "How? Give him rhythm? I told him not to join the gospel chorus."

"But he likes it. Walker should give him a break."

"Some things you can't help people do. It's impossible," I said. *Just like you and Tommy can't help me to stand up before the writing club.*

Tommy walks over to us and his round face is sagging.

"What did Walker say?" I ask.

"He'd pull me out if I don't keep still." I feel sorry for him. His father and mother walk in. It would be embarrassing if he got thrown out of the chorus while his parents are watching.

My father is nowhere in sight.

"I have an idea, but I have to ask Mr. Walker," Deidre says suddenly and runs over to him. Walker's face stretches into a long frown as he nods impatiently and throws his hands up in the air like he's so frustrated he'd agree to anything.

Deidre dashes back over to me, her face a dazzling smile. "Walker said I could stand on the other side of Tommy and you and I sway him in the right direction when he goes off."

"Walker's letting you sing in the boys' section?"

"It doesn't matter. I know my part. I'll sing when the sopranos do."

"Dee, this ain't gonna work."

"Trust me."

"Why do you always have to be so helpful? We're gonna look like Big Black, Big White and the Little Spasm."

Deidre throws her head back and laughs. Any other girl would get angry.

The audience is full and Walker springs up to the podium like he's on a pogo stick. I start to sweat when I see my mother walk in. She'll have plenty to say—especially about Tommy swaying in the wrong direction. I take a last look around for my father and decide to forget it. I hope the note and the poem got lost in the mail.

We sing "Oh Happy Day," then we belt out "Joy, Joy," and if Tommy even twitches Deidre pulls his robe. He's motionless. We don't sway in those, just a slight rocking back and forth. "I'll Fly Away" is next and my heart beat speeds up. Thanks to Deidre we'll end up looking like three jerks.

He doesn't move for the first few bars, but when we sing "I'll fly away, oh glory, I'll fly away," I feel him twitch and I peek over at him. His eyes are closed, his head thrown back. He's getting ready to break out. Deidre grabs his arm and pulls him in her direction and I grab his other arm. We sway and rock him through the song. The boy has heart.

Suddenly the audience starts to clap and sing along with us. I see Deidre's little head bobbing on the other side of Tommy as she pulls him toward her. The place is rocking and as long as me and Deidre sway Tommy in the right direction, he's moving in time to the music. Walker indicates for us to take another chorus, and Deidre must have gotten some kind of spirit because she lets Tommy go, starts clapping faster and Tommy jerks away from me and claps in his own time making herky-jerky movements. Walker is smiling and bouncing up and down. Doesn't he see Tommy? I guess all of us are swept up by the smiling, clapping, singing audience.

Tommy is all smiles when the concert ends and everyone compliments us. Mr. Walker is all smiles too. He says privately to me and Deidre while Tommy is shaking hands, "Thank you, Mr. Lamont and Miss Deidre. That was a touch of genius." Walker hadn't even seen Tommy going off in his own direction. Perhaps it didn't matter. People see what they want to see in the end.

My mother is running her mouth to a group of parents and she's pointing in my direction. I don't have to hear her to know exactly what she's saying. "That's my son over there. He's a wonderful singer." I see Mrs. Mackey, but I don't want to speak to her now. I'm not blaming her or anything like that for making me send the poem to my father, but I don't want her gushing over me. I also see Deidre heading for the door with her mother and I follow them so that I can tell Deidre good night. When I push open the door I'm shocked.

My father is standing there in his dusty blue pants and shirt, looking confused, like he doesn't know what to do with himself. "Lamont, I'm sorry I missed the concert. I couldn't get away from the garage in time. I heard the last song. I hear you, son. You know what I mean?" He shrugged his shoulders and looked at me kind of pitiful. Like I said, he is a man of few words.

I thought Mrs. Mackey would faint when I raised my hand. I felt the sweaty beads popping out on my forehead, but I was determined this time. Tommy gave me the thumbs-up sign and a few words of wisdom. "When people make you nervous, just think they go to the bathroom same as you do."

Deidre's dazzling smile dried up some of the sweat on my forehead. I walked slowly to the front of the room and reminded myself that my words, perhaps, got my father to show up even if he missed the concert. And even if my mother said, "Just showing up after everything is over isn't good enough."

The other kids laughed and teased as I knew they would, but it was the kind of teasing that friends do to each other. "I don't believe it," one of the rappers said. "It took two years for you to get up here in front of us?"

The athlete shouted, "Man, sit your big self down, don't nobody want to hear what you have to say now."

I knew that they would goof on me. I deserved it for being afraid to show myself. I felt the sweat popping out again and thought about Tommy swinging to his own time and no one noticing him, because Tommy didn't notice. I smiled at *The Most Popular Girl in the World* and *Moonface*. Though they remained in their seats, it was like they stood on either side of me. Helping me to sway and not feel like a hulk who wanted to break into little pieces. I'd start from the beginning. After I went home the night of the concert, I'd finished "A Safe Space." As I read I began to feel so comfortable in the unnaturalness of me.

> *Mama, Papa*
> *Once a safe space in*
> *a boy's life. When did it start?*
> *Muffled sounds in the night*
> *Cries you couldn't hide*
> *Hate seeping through*
> *the cracks in the walls*
> *oozing out of ceilings*
> *sliding under doors.*
> *You know everything, yet you*
> *couldn't make him stay?*
> *And you*
> *Did you have to leave?*
> *Do you detest the sight of me and her?*
> *Is that why you hid behind newspapers and*
> *in front of televisions?*
> *She misses you too, but never speaks your name,*

or tells me why you left us.
Alone.
Your name is now "Your Father."
"Your Father hasn't called."
"Your Father isn't here."
"Your Father doesn't care—
You act just like Your Father."

But I am me, not really alone.

I have found
A Safe Space of my own.

Lewis Carroll

A Mad Tea-party

from *Alice's Adventures in Wonderland*

After falling asleep, Alice falls down a rabbit hole, becomes very small, and meets many strange creatures, such as the Mad Hatter, a Dormouse, and the March Hare, who invite her to join them at tea.

THERE WAS A TABLE set out under a tree in front of the house, and the March Hare and the Hatter were having tea at it; a Dormouse was sitting between them, fast asleep, and the other two were using it as a cushion, resting their elbows on it, and talking over its head. "Very uncomfortable for the Dormouse," thought Alice; "only as it's asleep, I suppose it doesn't mind."

The table was a large one, but the three were all crowded together at one corner of it. "No room! No room!" they cried out when they saw Alice coming. "There's *plenty* of room!" said Alice indignantly, and she sat down in a large arm-chair at one end of the table.

"Have some wine," the March Hare said in an encouraging tone.

Alice looked all round the table, but there was nothing on it but tea. "I don't see any wine," she remarked.

"There isn't any," said the March Hare.

"Then it wasn't very civil of you to offer it," said Alice angrily.

"It wasn't very civil of you to sit down without being invited," said the March Hare.

"I didn't know it was *your* table," said Alice: "it's laid for a great many more than three."

"Your hair wants cutting," said the Hatter. He had been looking at Alice for some time with great curiosity, and this was his first speech.

"You should learn not to make personal remarks," Alice said with some severity: "It's very rude."

The Hatter opened his eyes very wide on hearing this; but all he *said* was "Why is a raven like a writing-desk?"

"Come, we shall have some fun now!" thought Alice. "I'm glad they've begun asking riddles—I believe I can guess that," she added aloud.

"Do you mean that you think you can find out the answer to it?" said the March Hare.

"Exactly so," said Alice.

"Then you should say what you mean," the March Hare went on.

"I do," Alice hastily replied; "at least—at least I mean what I say—that's the same thing, you know."

"Not the same thing a bit!" said the Hatter. "Why, you might just as well say that 'I see what I eat' is the same thing as 'I eat what I see'!"

"You might just as well say," added the March Hare, "that 'I like what I get' is the same thing as 'I get what I like'!"

"You might just as well say," added the Dormouse, which seemed to be talking in its sleep, "that 'I breathe when I sleep' is the same thing as 'I sleep when I breathe'!"

"It *is* the same thing with you," said the Hatter, and here the conversation dropped, and the party sat silent for a minute, while Alice thought over all she could remember about ravens and writing-desks, which wasn't much.

The Hatter was the first to break the silence. "What day of the month is it?" he said, turning to Alice: he had taken his watch out of his pocket, and was looking at it uneasily, shaking it every now and then, and holding it to his ear.

Alice considered a little, and then said "The fourth."

"Two days wrong!" sighed the Hatter. "I told you butter wouldn't suit the works!" he added, looking angrily at the March Hare.

"It was the *best* butter," the March Hare meekly replied.

"Yes, but some crumbs must have got in as well," the Hatter grumbled: "you shouldn't have put it in with the bread-knife."

The March Hare took the watch and looked at it gloomily: then he dipped it into his cup of tea, and looked at it again: but he could think of nothing better to say than his first remark, "It was the *best* butter, you know."

Alice had been looking over his shoulder with some curiosity. "What a funny watch!" she remarked. "It tells the day of the month, and doesn't tell what o'clock it is!"

"Why should it?" muttered the Hatter. "Does *your* watch tell you what year it is?"

"Of course not," Alice replied very readily: "but that's because it stays the same year for such a long time together."

"Which is just the case with *mine*," said the Hatter.

Alice felt dreadfully puzzled. The Hatter's remark seemed to her to have no sort of meaning in it, and yet it was certainly English. "I don't quite understand you," she said, as politely as she could.

"The Dormouse is asleep again," said the Hatter, and he poured a little hot tea upon its nose.

The Dormouse shook its head impatiently, and said, without opening its eyes, "Of course, of course: just what I was going to remark myself."

"Have you guessed the riddle yet?" the Hatter said, turning to Alice again.

"No, I give it up," Alice replied. "What's the answer?"

"I haven't the slightest idea," said the Hatter.

"Nor I," said the March Hare.

Alice sighed wearily. "I think you might do something better with the time," she said, "than wasting it in asking riddles that have no answers."

"If you knew Time as well as I do," said the Hatter, "you wouldn't talk about wasting *it*. It's *him*."

"I don't know what you mean," said Alice.

"Of course you don't!" the Hatter said, tossing his head contemptuously. "I dare say you never even spoke to Time!"

"Perhaps not," Alice cautiously replied; "but I know I have to beat time when I learn music."

"Ah! That accounts for it," said the Hatter. "He wo'n't stand beating. Now, if you only kept on good terms with him, he'd do almost anything you liked with the clock. For instance, suppose it were nine o'clock in the morning, just time to begin lessons: you'd only have to whisper a hint to Time, and round goes the clock in a twinkling! Half-past one, time for dinner!"

("I only wish it was," the March Hare said to itself in a whisper.)

"That would be grand, certainly," said Alice thoughtfully; "but then—I shouldn't be hungry for it, you know."

"Not at first, perhaps," said the Hatter: "but you could keep it to half-past one as long as you liked."

"Is that the way *you* manage?" Alice asked.

The Hatter shook his head mournfully. "Not I!" he replied. "We quarreled last March——just before *he* went mad, you know——" (pointing with his teaspoon at the March Hare,) "——it was at the great concert given by the Queen of Hearts, and I had to sing

> *'Twinkle twinkle, little bat!*
> *How I wonder what you're at!'*

You know the song, perhaps?"

"I've heard something like it," said Alice,

"It goes on, you know," the Hatter continued, "in this way:—

> *'Up above the world you fly,*
> *Like a tea-tray in the sky.*
>   *Twinkle, twinkle——' "*

Here the Dormouse shook itself, and began singing in its sleep *"Twinkle, twinkle, twinkle, twinkle——"* and went on so long that they had to pinch it to make it stop.

"Well, I'd hardly finished the first verse," said the Hatter, "when the Queen bawled out 'He's murdering the time! Off with his head!'"

"How dreadfully savage!" exclaimed Alice.

"And ever since that," the Hatter went on in a mournful tone, "he wo'n't do a thing I ask! It's always six o'clock now."

A bright idea came into Alice's head. "Is that the reason so many tea-things are put out here?" she asked.

"Yes, that's it," said the Hatter with a sigh: "it's always tea-time, and we've no time to wash the things between whiles."

"Then you keep moving round, I suppose?" said Alice.

"Exactly so," said the Hatter: "as the things get used up."

"But what happens when you come to the beginning again?" Alice ventured to ask.

"Suppose we change the subject," the March Hare interrupted, yawning. "I'm getting tired of this. I vote the young lady tells us a story."

"I'm afraid I don't know one," said Alice, rather alarmed at the proposal.

"Then the Dormouse shall!" they both cried. "Wake up, Dormouse!" And they pinched it on both sides at once.

The Dormouse slowly opened its eyes. "I wasn't asleep," it said in a hoarse, feeble voice, "I heard every word you fellows were saying."

"Tell us a story!" said the March Hare.

"Yes, please do!" pleaded Alice.

"And be quick about it," added the Hatter, "or you'll be asleep again before it's done."

"Once upon a time there were three little sisters," the Dormouse began in a great hurry: "and their names were Elsie, Lacie, and Tillie; and they lived at the bottom of a well——"

"What did they live on?" said Alice, who always took a great interest in questions of eating and drinking.

"They lived on treacle," said the Dormouse, after thinking a minute to two.

"They couldn't have done that, you know," Alice gently remarked. "They'd have been ill."

"So they were," said the Dormouse; "*very* ill."

Alice tried a little to fancy to herself what such an extraordinary way of living would be like, but it puzzled her too much: so she went on: "But why did they live at the bottom of the well?"

"Take some more tea," the March Hare said to Alice, very earnestly.

"I've had nothing yet," Alice replied in an offended tone: "so I can't take more."

"You mean you can't take *less*," said the Hatter: "it's very easy to take *more* than nothing."

"Nobody asked *your* opinion," said Alice.

"Who's making personal remarks now?" the Hatter asked triumphantly.

Alice did not quite know what to say to this: so she helped herself to some tea and bread-and-butter, and then turned to the Dormouse, and repeated her question, "Why did they live at the bottom of a well?"

The Dormouse again took a minute or two to think about it, and then said "It was a treacle-well."

"There's no such thing!" Alice was beginning very angrily, but the Hatter and the March Hare went "Sh! Sh!" and the Dormouse sulkily remarked "If you ca'n't be civil, you'd better finish the story for yourself."

"No, please go on!" Alice said very humbly. "I wo'n't interrupt you again. I dare say there may be *one*."

"One, indeed!" said the Dormouse indignantly. However, he consented to go on. "And so these three little sisters—they were learning to draw, you know——"

"What did they draw?" said Alice, quite forgetting her promise.

"Treacle," said the Dormouse, without considering at all, this time.

"I want a clean cup," interrupted the Hatter: "let's all move one place on."

He moved on as he spoke, and the Dormouse followed him: the March Hare moved into the Dormouse's place, and Alice rather unwillingly took the place of the March Hare. The Hatter was the only one who got any advantage from the change; and Alice was a good deal worse off than before, as the March Hare had just upset the milk-jug into his plate.

Alice did not wish to offend the Dormouse again, so she began very cautiously: "But I don't understand. Where did they draw the treacle from?"

"You can draw water out of a water-well," said the Hatter; "so I should think you could draw treacle out of a treacle-well—eh, stupid?"

"But they were *in* the well," Alice said to the Dormouse, not choosing to notice this last remark.

"Of course they were," said the Dormouse: "well in."

This answer so confused poor Alice, that she let the Dormouse go on for some time without interrupting it.

"They were learning to draw," the Dormouse went on, yawning and rubbing his eyes, for it was getting very sleepy; "and they drew all manner of things—everything that begins with an M——"

"Why with an M?" said Alice.

"Why not?" said the March Hare.

Alice was silent.

The Dormouse had closed its eyes by this time, and was going off into a doze; but, on being pinched by the Hatter, it woke up again with a little shriek, and went on: "——that begins with an M, such as mouse-traps, and the moon, and memory, and muchness—you know you say things are 'much of a muchness'—did you ever see such a thing as a drawing of a muchness?"

"Really, now you ask me," said Alice, very much confused, "I don't think——"

"Then you shouldn't talk," said the Hatter.

This piece of rudeness was more than Alice could bear: she got up in great disgust, and walked off: the Dormouse fell asleep instantly, and neither of the others took the least notice of her going, though she looked back once or twice, half hoping that they would call after her: the last time she saw them, they were trying to put the Dormouse into the teapot.

"At any rate I'll never go *there* again!" said Alice, as she picked her way through the wood. "It's the stupidest tea-party I ever was at in all my life!"

Sea Turtles

*Nadia's fascination with the turtles is shared by people
all around the world. By presenting facts both odd
and ordinary, this selection may encourage others to
help keep the turtles' beaches safe.*

Habitat and Distribution.

A. Distribution.
Sea turtles are found in warm and temperate seas throughout the world.

B. Habitat.
Adults of most species are found in shallow, coastal waters, bays, la-
goons, and estuaries. Some also venture into the open seas. Juveniles of
some species may be found in bays and estuaries, as well as at sea.

C. Migration.
1. Migration habits differ not only among species but also among different populations of the same species. Some sea turtle populations nest and
feed in the same general areas; others migrate great distances.

    a. Green sea turtle populations migrate primarily along the coasts
    from nesting to feeding grounds. However, some populations will
    travel 2,094 km (1,300 miles) across the Atlantic Ocean from the
    Ascension Island nesting grounds to the Brazilian coast feeding
    grounds.

    b. Black sea turtles migrate along the coast from breeding areas to
    feeding grounds between the northern and southern extremes of
    their distribution range.

c. Loggerheads leave foraging areas and travel on breeding migrations that range from a few to thousands of kilometers (1 kilometer = 0.62 miles).

d. Kemp's ridley turtles follow two major routes in the Gulf of Mexico: one northward to the Mississippi area, the other southward to the Campeche Bank, near the Yucatan Peninsula.

e. Populations of olive ridleys have been observed in large flotillas traveling between feeding and nesting grounds in the Eastern Pacific and Indian Oceans.

f. Hawksbill migration studies have been limited. Evidence suggests that some hawksbill populations show cyclic nesting migrations. Other researches have documented nonmigratory and short-distance migratory populations.

g. Flatbacks move from their nesting grounds on the northern coast of Australia and islands to feeding grounds in shallow waters of northeastern Australia. Distance covered ranges from 215 to 1,300 km (134 – 807 miles).

h. Leatherbacks have the longest migration of all sea turtles. They have been found more than 4,831 km (3,000 miles) from their nesting beaches.

2. The most common method used to track free-ranging sea turtles is flipper tagging. Although this method yields information on migration destinations, it does not reveal travel routes.

3. Recently radio, sonic, and satellite tracking have been successful in monitoring sea turtle movements.

4. Hubbs-Sea World Research Institute has developed a radio transmitter harness for leatherback turtles. Its design allows secure attachment of a transmitter without affecting turtle mobility. The harness was designed to release within several months.

D. Population.
1. Total population figures are often unknown because juvenile and male sea turtles do not come ashore and are difficult to count.

2. Population data are usually based on the numbers of adult females that come ashore to nest. Even then, the numbers are ambiguous— some females nest every two or three years, some may nest more than once on the same beach in a season, and some females will visit more than one nesting beach in a season.

3. Researches rely more upon the changing numbers of nesting females from year to year to determine population trends of increasing or decreasing numbers. Because broad year-to-year fluctuations in numbers of nesting females make short-term data misleading, surveys of a decade or less may be insufficient to determine a population trend.

 a. The Kemp's ridley is the most endangered sea turtle. In 1947, 92,000 nests were estimated. The numbers have been declining dramatically since then. Surveys conducted between 1978 and 1988 indicated an average of about 800 nests per year. Since 1978, the trend shows the number of nests have been declining at about 14 nests per year. The total number of nesting females may be as low as 350 on beaches where tens of thousands of Kemp's ridley used to nest.

 b. Nesting populations of green and black sea turtles have not been surveyed long enough for determination of trends. However, qualitative observations during visits over several years suggest a heavy decline.

 c. The major loggerhead nesting grounds are located in the southeastern U.S. Population trends of loggerheads show a decline in nesting areas of Georgia and South Carolina, but no decline or a possible increase in southern Florida Atlantic areas. More years of nesting data and population biology studies are needed to assess the Florida trends.

 d. There are probably several hundred thousand adult female olive ridleys. The olive ridley is the most abundant sea turtle in the world. In 1991, an estimated 610,000 turtles nested in a single week on a beach in India.

 e. Very little data are available on hawksbill populations. Estimation of population sizes of nesting females is difficult by aerial assessment: tracks in the sand do not last long and are difficult to see, and nests are often obscured by beach vegetation.

f. Current population numbers for flatback turtles are not known; however, because of its restricted distribution, the flatback is the most vulnerable of all sea turtles to any habitat change or over-exploitation.

g. There are probably less than 115,000 adult female leatherbacks worldwide. There are too few records to predict trends; however, the numbers do not appear to be declining.

Physical Characteristics.

A. Size.
Adult males and females are equal in size.

1. Green sea turtles reach about 78 to 112 cm (31-44 in.) and 68 to 186 kg (150-410 lb.). The largest individual collected was 1.5 m (5 ft.) and 395 kg (871 lb.).

2. Black sea turtles reach about 59 to 117 cm (23-46 in.) and 42 to 126 kg (93-278 lb.).

3. The Kemp's ridley and olive ridley are the smallest species, and reach about 55 to 65 cm (22-30 in.) and 30 to 50 kg (66-110 lb.).

4. Loggerheads reach about 82 to 105 cm (32-41 in.) and 66 to 101 kg (146-223 lb.).

5. Hawksbills reach about 53 to 114 cm (21-45 in.) and 27 to 86 kg (60-190 lb.).

6. Flatbacks reach about 81 to 97 cm (32-38 in.) and 60 to 84 kg (132-185 lb.).

7. The leatherback is the largest of all living sea turtles. Mature leatherbacks reach about 1.2 to 1.9 m (4-6 ft.) and 200 to 506 kg (441-1,116 lb.). The largest leatherback recorded was 916 kg (2,019 lb.).

B. Body shape.
Sea turtles are characterized by a large, streamlined shell and nonretractile head and limbs.

C. Coloration.
1. Depending on the species, sea turtles ranges in color. They may be olive-green, yellow, greenish-brown, or black.

2. The green sea turtle gets its name from the color of its body fat.

D. Flippers.
1. A sea turtle cannot retract its limbs under its shell as a land turtle can.

2. Flippers are adapted for swimming. Sea turtles are awkward and vulnerable on land.

3. Foreflippers are long and paddlelike.
   a. Long digits are fused throughout the flipper.
   b. Only one or two claws are present on each foreflipper.
   c. A sea turtle swims with powerful winglike beats of its foreflippers.

4. Hind flippers serve as rudders, stabilizing and directing the animal as it swims. The hind flippers of some species are quite dexterous in digging nests in the sand.

E. Head.
1. A sea turtle cannot retract its head under its shell as a land turtle can.

2. Sea turtles have large upper eyelids that provide protection for their eyes.

3. Sea turtles do not have an external ear opening.

4. Like other turtles, sea turtles lack teeth. Jaw shape varies among species. Each species has a jaw shape adapted for its diet.

F. Shell.

1. The large, bony shell provides protection from predation and abrasion.

2. In all species except the leatherback, the shell is covered with a layer of horny plates called scutes.

a. Scutes are firm but flexible, not brittle.

b. Scientists can identify sea turtle species by the number and pattern of scutes.

c. The leatherback turtle has a thick and oil-suffused skin, which is an excellent insulator allowing this species to venture into colder waters.

3. The dorsal (top) side of the shell is called the *carapace.*

a. Depending on species, the adult carapace ranges in shape from oval to heart-shaped.

b. In all species except the leatherback, the bony shell is composed of broadened, fused ribs, and the backbone is attached to the carapace.

c. The leatherback's carapace is composed largely of cartilage raised into prominent longitudinal ridges. A layer of thousands of small dermal bones lies just below the leathery skin.

4. The ventral (bottom) side of the shell is called the *plastron.*

G. Sexual dimorphism.

1. Male and female sea turtles do not differ externally until they approach maturity.

2. Adult males have longer, thicker tails, because the male reproductive organ is housed in the base of the tail. In males, the tail may extend beyond the hind flippers.

3. On some species, the claws on the foreflippers of males are elongated and curved, which may help in grasping the females' shells during mating.

Diet and Eating Habits.

A. Food preferences and resources.
Diet varies with species. Sea turtles may be *carnivorous* (meat eating), *herbivorous* (plant eating), or *omnivorous* (eating both meat and plants). The jaw structure of many species indicates their diet.

1. Green and black sea turtles have finely serrated jaws adapted for a vegetarian diet of sea grasses and algae. In adulthood, they are the only herbivorous sea turtles, but in an aquarium environment all sea turtle species can be maintained on a carnivorous diet.

2. Loggerheads' and ridleys' jaws are adapted for crushing and grinding. Their diet consists primarily of crabs, mollusks, shrimp, jellyfish, and vegetation.

3. A hawksbill has a narrow head with jaws meeting at an acute angle, adapted for getting food from crevices in coral reefs. They eat sponges, tunicates, shrimps, and squids.

4. Leatherbacks have delicate scissorlike jaws that would be damaged by anything other than their normal diet of jellyfish, tunicates, and other soft-bodied animals. The mouth cavity and throat are lined with *papillae* (spinelike projections) pointed backward to help them swallow soft foods.

5. Researchers continue to study the feeding habits of flatbacks. There is evidence that they are opportunistic feeders that eat seaweeds, cuttlefish, and sea cucumbers.

B. Eating habits.
Some species change eating habits as they age. For instance, green sea turtles are mainly carnivorous from hatchling until juvenile size; they then progressively shift to an herbivorous diet.

Hatching and Hatchlings.

A. Incubation.
1. Incubation time varies with species, clutch size, and temperature and humidity in the nest.

2. The incubation time for most species is 45 to 70 days.

3. Research indicates that the sex of an embryo is determined sometime after fertilization, as the embryo develops, and may be temperature dependent. Lower nest temperatures produce more males; higher temperatures produce more females.

B. Hatching.
1. Sea turtles hatch throughout the year but mostly in summer.

2. Hatchlings use a *caruncle* (temporary egg tooth) to help break open the shell.

3. After hatching, the young turtles may take three to seven days to dig their way to the surface.

4. Hatchlings usually wait until night to emerge from the nest. Emerging at night reduces exposure to daytime predators. They leave the nest and head to the water in groups. Studies have shown that some nests will produce hatchlings on more than one night.

C. Reaching the ocean.
1. There are several theories as to how hatchlings find the sea.

    a. Hatchlings may discriminate light intensities and head for the greater light intensity of the open horizon.

    b. During the crawl to the sea, the hatchling may set an internal magnetic compass, which it uses for navigation away from the beach.

2. When the hatchling reaches the surf, it dives into a wave and rides the undertow out to sea.

a. A "swim frenzy" of continuous swimming takes place for about 24 to 48 hours after the hatchling enters the water.

b. This frantic activity gets the young turtle into deeper water, where it is less vulnerable to predators.

c. There have been reports of swimming hatchlings diving straight down when birds and even airplanes appear overhead. This diving behavior may be a behavioral adaptation for avoiding predation by birds.

D. The first year.

1. During the first year, many species of sea turtles are rarely seen. This first year is known as the "lost year."

2. Researchers generally agree that most hatchlings spend their first few years living an oceanic existence before appearing in coastal areas. Although the migratory patterns of the young turtles during the first year has long been a puzzle, most researchers believe that they ride prevailing surface currents, situating themselves in floating seaweed where they are camouflaged and where they can find food.

3. Research suggests that flatback hatchlings do not go through an oceanic phase. Evidence shows that the young turtles remain inshore following the initial swim frenzy. Most remain within 15 km (9.3 miles) of land.

Longevity and Causes of Death.

A. Longevity.

Scientists are still researching sea turtle longevity. Once sea turtles reach sexual maturity, they may have an estimated reproductive life of about 30 years. Given that some species reach maturity at 50 years, an 80-year lifespan is feasible.

B. Aging.

Currently there is not an adequate method of aging sea turtles. The most accepted method, aside from observing a turtle from the time it hatches, is to study rings of the scales on the carapace and plastron. Scientists count the rings and use a mathematical formula to estimate a turtle's age.

C. Natural predators.
1. Adult sea turtles have few predators, mostly large sharks. Tiger sharks, in particular, are known for eating sea turtles. Killer whales have been known to prey on leatherback turtles.

2. Fishes, dogs, seabirds, raccoons, ghost crabs, and other predators prey on eggs and hatchlings. More than 90% of hatchlings are eaten by these predators.

3. Flatback turtle nests are susceptible to predation by monitor lizards, dingoes, and introduced foxes.

D. Fibropapillomas.
Green sea turtles and black sea turtles may develop lobed tumorlike growths (fibropapillomas) on the skin. These growths can result in reduced vision, obstruction of normal swimming and feeding, and increased susceptibility to secondary parasitism and infection.

E. Human impact.
1. Nesting areas are becoming scarce due to beach development and disturbances. Kemp's ridleys only nest on one beach in the entire world: on a remote beach in Mexico near the village of Rancho Nuevo (about 161 km, or 100 miles, south of the Texas border). In 1947, scientists witnessed an arribada of more than 40,000 Kemp's ridley turtles in one day. In the 1960s, numbers were reduced to less than 5,000 turtles. In 1973, the largest arribada contained only 200 individuals.

2. Although the population of olive ridley sea turtles is the most abundant in the world, their major nesting beach at Gahirmatha in Orissa, India, is in jeopardy. The Government of India is planning to develop a major fishing port and processing plant 10 km (6.2 miles) from the critical nesting beach. More sea turtles nest on this beach than on any other beach in the world.

3. Nesting females and hatchlings are disturbed by the presence of trash on nesting beaches. If trash impedes its crawl up the beach, a female returns to the sea instead of nesting.

4. The noise and activity of people on the beach also may cause females to return to the sea instead of nesting.

5. Some sea turtles die when they ingest trash. Leatherbacks are especially susceptible to ingesting plastic, mistaking it for jellyfish.

6. Thousands of sea turtles drown in shrimp nets each year. Sea turtles forage in waters where commercial shrimpers trawl. In 1947, 5,000 U.S. shrimping trawlers worked in the Gulf of Mexico. That number increased to 15,000 full-time and 40,000 part-time trawlers by 1989.

7. Artificial lighting on beaches may misrepresent the time of day to turtles attempting to nest. Most turtles are nocturnal nesters, and to a turtle that has not yet come ashore to nest, a brightly lighted beach may signify daylight and inhibit nesting.

8. Hatchlings can become disoriented by city and street lights when trying to find the surf. Many young turtles actually head away from the ocean and toward parking lots. These animals may be eaten by predators or crushed by cars. Some die from exposure.

9. Some people illegally collect turtle eggs for food and for their alleged aphrodisiac effects.

10. Sea turtles are hunted (illegally in this country and in some cases legally elsewhere) for their meat and shells, which are used to make combs, eyeglass frames, aphrodisiacs, and curios. The fat of green sea turtles, boiled with cartilage called *calipee*, made a popular soup, which led to the decline in green sea turtle population numbers.

11. Deforestation may indirectly threaten sea turtle nests. Costa Rica has one of the highest deforestation rates in the world. Some researchers fear that without the forest to draw up ground water, the water table will rise beneath the beaches and drown nests.

12. Propeller and collision injuries from boats are not uncommon. These types of injuries are more frequent in areas with a high level of recreational boating, such as South Florida, the Florida Keys, and the United States Virgin Islands.

Conservation.

A. Legal protection for sea turtles.

1. All eight species of sea turtles are listed as threatened or endangered on the U.S. Endangered and Threatened Wildlife and Plants List. It is illegal to harm, or in any way interfere with, a sea turtle or its eggs.

2. The Convention on International Trade in Endangered Species of Wild Fauna and Flora (CITES) is an international treaty developed in 1973 to regulate trade in certain wildlife species. CITES protects all species of sea turtles. The U.S. and 115 other countries have banned the import or export of sea turtle products.

B. Turtle Excluder Device.

1. At a cost of millions of dollars, the National Marine Fisheries Service developed the Turtle Excluder Device (TED).

2. The TED is a small, metal grid trapdoor inside a trawling net that allows shrimp to pass to the back while the turtles escape to safety before becoming entrapped or entangled.

3. Since 1989, federal law requires that this device be installed on the nets of all U.S. fishing trawlers working in areas populated by sea turtles.

C. Protecting nests.

1. Nests can be protected from predators by placing screens over them. Eggs laid too close to the water or in erosion zones can be relocated to safer areas.

2. In a bold conservation program, the townspeople of a small Costa Rican village are allowed to gather eggs laid during the first two

nights of each olive ridley arribada. Scientists have calculated that a controlled harvest would leave enough protected eggs to rejuvenate the population (in one nesting season, 20 to 30 million olive ridley eggs may be laid in this beach village) while allowing villagers to maintain a livelihood. The program has the potential to stop poachers of other eggs on other beaches by keeping the prices of the "legal" eggs too low for poachers to compete.

D. Lighting.
Although eliminating beach lighting would be the most effective way to reduce disorientation of hatchlings, studies have shown that low pressure sodium vapor lights have a lesser effect on loggerhead and green sea turtle hatchlings. Many beach communities have encouraged the use of these lights.

E. Wildlife refuges.
1. Legislation is underway to allocate government funding for the Archie Carr National Wildlife Refuge on the east coast of Florida, between Melbourne Beach and Vero Beach. Full protection of the refuge would cost a total of $90 million dollars, of which $50 million would come from state and local sources. As of 1994, federal funding has reached $7 million.

a. This 33-km (20.5-mile) section of beach is the most important nesting site for loggerheads in the Western Hemisphere.

b. The refuge is the most important nesting beach in the United States for the green sea turtle.

c. The refuge also is considered prime real estate for commercial development, making government funding essential to its preservation.

2. The governments of Nicaragua and Costa Rica have established, and are striving to expand, national parks and biological reserves where sea turtles forage and nest. Tortuguero, Costa Rica, maintains the largest green sea turtle rookery in the Caribbean. Local economics is no longer based on turtle harvests, but on tourism. More than 15,000 visitors are expected each year.

F. Managing sex ratios.

Most conservationists believe that abundant nesting females are desirable to rejuvenate sea turtle populations. Researchers with Reproductive Sciences, Inc. and Reptile Conservation International have developed, and are patenting, a technique of applying an estrogen solution onto eggs to produce a higher number of females under normal incubation.

G. In zoological environments.

1. Having sea turtles at marine zoological parks provides an opportunity for the public to learn, up-close, about these animals and how human activities may impact their survival.

2. In the protected environment of a marine zoological park, scientists can examine aspects of sea turtle biology that are difficult or impossible to study in the wild.

3. Sea World of Florida treats numerous green and loggerhead sea turtles each year.

    a. Sea turtles often are brought in after a cold weather snap. Low water temperatures cause a sea turtle's metabolism to slow—the hypothermic turtles become sluggish and are unable to feed. Marine patrol officers may find the turtles floating at the surface of the water in a semi-dormant state.

    b. In December 1989, 95 hypothermic green sea turtles were rescued from Florida's Merritt Island. These turtles were housed in recovery pools at Sea World of Florida for about 10 weeks. Once the weather warmed up, the turtles were released in the same area that they were rescued.

    c. Sea World has rescued other sea turtles with injuries resulting from entanglement, motorboat collisions, ocean dredging, or ingestion of non-food items.

4. Data gathered through the Sea World Animal Rescue and Rehabilitation Program and similar programs can help scientists more accurately assess and recommend sea turtle population management programs in the wild.

compiled by
Jack Canfield,
Mark Victor
Hansen,
Kimberly
Kirberger

from
Chicken Soup for the Teenage Soul II

These anecdotes, written by teens and based on their own experiences, reveal acts of neighborliness and kindness similar to the ways in which Nadia and her friends interact to help one another.

An A for Mrs. B

Karina Snow

I WAS SITTING NEXT TO MISSY in my ninth-grade world history class when Mrs. Bartlett announced a new project. In groups, we were to create a newspaper around the culture we were studying.

On a piece of paper, we wrote the names of three friends we wanted in our group. After collecting all the requests, Mrs. B. informed us that she would take into consideration the names we chose and would let us know the results the next day. I had no doubt I would get the group of my choice. There were only a handful of sociably decent people in the class, and Missy was one of them. I knew we had chosen each other.

The next day, I anxiously awaited the class. After the bell rang, Missy and I stopped talking as Mrs. B called for our attention. She started to call out names. When she reached group three, Missy's name was called. *So I'm in group three*, I thought. The second, third and fourth members of the group were called. My name was not included. There had to be some mistake!

Then I heard it. The last group: "Mauro, Juliette, Rachel, Karina." I could feel the tears well in my eyes. How could I face being in that group—the boy who barely spoke English, the one girl who was always covered by skirts that went down to her ankles, and the other girl who wore weird clothes. Oh, how badly I wanted to be with my friends.

I fought back tears as I walked up to Mrs. B. She looked at me and knew what I was there for. I was determined to convince her I should be in the "good" group. "Why . . . ?" I started.

She gently placed a hand on my shoulder. "I know what you want, Karina," she said, "but your group needs you. I need you to help them get a passing grade on this assignment. Only you can help them."

I was stunned. I was humbled. I was amazed. She had seen something in me I hadn't seen.

"Will you help them?" she asked.

I stood straighter. "Yes," I replied. I couldn't believe it came out of my mouth, but it did. I had committed.

As I bravely walked to where the others in my group sat, I could hear the laughter from my friends. I sat down and we started. Different newspaper columns were assigned according to interests. We did research. Halfway through the week, I felt myself enjoying the company of these three misfits. There was no need for pretending—I grew sincerely interested in learning something about them.

Mauro, I found out, was struggling with the English language and his lack of friends. Juliette was also alone, because people didn't understand that she was only allowed to wear long skirts or dresses because of her religion. Rachel, who had requested to do the fashion column, wanted to be a fashion designer. She had a whole barrel of unique ideas. What a walk in another person's shoes did for me! They weren't misfits, just people that no one cared enough about to try to understand—except Mrs. B. Her insight, vision, and thoughtfulness brought out the potential in four of her students.

I don't recall what the newspaper's headline was or even the culture we wrote about, but I did learn something that week. I was given a chance to see other people in a new light. I was given the opportunity to see in myself a potential that inspired my actions in later years. I learned that who we are is more important than what we are or seem to be.

After that semester ended, I always received a friendly hello from my group. And I was always genuinely happy to see them.

Mrs. B. gave us an A on that assignment. We should have handed it right back, for she was the one who truly deserved it.

Change for a Dollar
Bonnie Maloney

> *Make yourself a blessing to someone. Your kind smile or pat on the back just might pull someone back from the edge.*
>
> Carmelia Elliot

ALL HE WANTED WAS SOME JUICE. As tables full of high school students sat in Cafeteria B2 on that cloudy afternoon, he was thirsty. We sat near yet away from him, fixing our hair and worrying about the test next period we hadn't studied for. He was far away from our world, yet forced to be a part of it.

He stood at the drink machine with purpose, fumbling through his fake leather wallet for some change. He came up with a wrinkled dollar bill, and nervously glanced back at his table where other students in his special needs class were sitting. With the coordination of a six-year-old, he tried to make the machine accept his money. After a few unsuccessful attempts, the snickers and comments began. People were laughing. Some were even throwing things at him. He began to quiver, and his eyes misted with tears. I saw him turn to sit down, defeated. But for some reason, he decided against it. He wasn't leaving until he got a drink.

With a determined expression, he continued to aimlessly thrust the dollar bill in the machine. Then something terrific happened. A popular senior rose from her seat, and with a look of genuine compassion, went over to the boy. She explained how the machine had a hard time accepting dollars, then gave him some change and showed him where to place it. The boy gave her his dollar and chose a flavor of fruit juice. Then the two walked off in different directions.

Although it was clear that they were from very different worlds, for one moment, they'd shared a real understanding. As I walked away from my lunch table that day, I looked at the boy. I remembered thinking how he and the dollar were very much alike. They both weren't accepted where the world said they were supposed to be. But just as the dollar had found a place in a caring girl's pocket, I was sure the boy would eventually find his, too.

So How Do You Boost an Ego?
Kirk Hill

If you treat an individual as he is, he will remain as he is. But if you treat him as if he were what he ought to be and could be, he will become what he ought to be and could be.

Goethe

MR. RICKMAN, OUR PSYCH TEACHER, doesn't give the kind of assignments other teachers do, such as read a thousand pages; answer the questions at the end of the chapter; work problems 47 through 856. He's more creative than that.

Mr. Rickman led up to last Thursday's assignment by saying that behavior is a means of communicating. " 'Actions speak louder than words' isn't just an empty phrase," he told us. "What people do tells you something about what they are feeling."

He paused a minute for that to sink in before he gave the assignment. "Now see if you can build up somebody, boost his or her ego enough that you notice a change in the way the person acts. We'll report the results in class next week."

When I got home from school that afternoon, my mom was really feeling sorry for herself. I could tell the minute I came in. Her hair was straggling around her face, her voice was whiney and she kept sighing while she got dinner. She didn't even speak to me when I came in. Since she didn't speak, I didn't either.

Dinner was pretty dreary. Dad wasn't any more talkative than

Mom and I were. I decided to try out my assignment. "Hey, Mom, you know that play the university drama club is putting on? Why don't you and Dad go tonight? I've heard it's really good."

"Can't make it tonight," Dad said. "Important meeting."

"Naturally," Mom said. Then I knew what was bugging her.

"Well then, how about going with me?" I asked. Right away, I wished I could take back the invitation. Imagine a high school kid being seen out in the evening with his mother!

Anyway, the invitation was hanging here in the air, and Mom said in an excited voice, "Really, Kirk?"

I swallowed a couple of times. "Sure. Why not?"

"But guys don't take their mothers out." Her voice was getting more pleasant all the time, and she pushed the straggles of hair up on top of her head.

"There's no law that says they can't," I told her. "You just go get ready. We're going out."

Mom started toward the sink with some dishes. Her steps were perky now instead of draggy.

"Kirk and I will take care of the dishes," Dad offered, and Mom even smiled at him.

"That was a nice thing for you to do," my dad said, after Mom left the kitchen. "You're a thoughtful son."

Thanks to psychology class, I thought gloomily.

Mom came back to the kitchen looking about five years younger than she had an hour earlier. "You're sure you don't have a date?" she asked, as if she still couldn't believe what was happening.

"I do now," I said. "C'mon, let's go."

That evening didn't turn out so badly after all. Most of my friends had more exciting things to do than watch a play. The ones who were there weren't at all startled to see me with my mom. By the end of the evening, she was genuinely happy, and I was feeling pretty good my-self. Not only had I aced a psych assignment, I had also learned a lot about boosting an ego.

Karen Fiser

Wheelchairs That Kneel Down Like Elephants

The speaker, who uses a wheelchair, dreams of
wonderful possibilities.

Last night I rode a tightrope
with my wheelchair. No net.
The night before, I left my body
on the steep ground with its pain.
5   I walked again by leaning,
elbows careless on the wind,
hitching myself along in light surprise.
Days I am heavy,
a clumsy bear on wheels,
10   bumping into things
and smiling, smiling. Nights
I invent new means of locomotion:
flying velocipedes, sailcars,
wheelchairs that kneel down
15   like elephants, carry me carefully
up the long stairs. Intricate
engines of need and night and air.